I0699956

IF I DENOUNCE MY ACCENT

SINDY FELIZ

PALMTREE PUBLISHING

Copyright © 2022 by Sindy Feliz

Library of Congress Control Number: 2022915769

Paperback ISBN: 979-8-9868027-0-1
Ebook ISBN: 979-8-9868027-1-8

Printed by Palmtree Publishing, in the United States of America.
First printing edition 2022.

"Independence didn't have to be exile."

\- Julia Alvarez

To all my Latina sisters who can never find their names on a keychain.

To my husband, you are home.

CHAPTER 1

MONEY-GROWING-ON-TREES PARADISE

I'm what they call an Island Girl, with beautiful big curly hair that behaves best when it encounters the sun. My hair has a mind of its own.

I remind myself of everything that defines my identity while I stare at my own reflection standing in front of the mirror, which hangs in a bedroom that is certainly more occupied than it should. I pretend I don't talk to myself too often, but who am I kidding? That's all I do. Especially after being hit with a wave of insecurities one day after school. I had to cheer myself up.

Everything hurts my self-esteem lately. Everything people say about me. *I started to question myself. Was my nose a socially acceptable size? Was my body composition desirable?* I began to think about my hair, and about the first time, I got it relaxed.

I was twelve years old when I lost my natural curl pattern. I begged my mom to let me relax it to smooth it. Everyone my age was getting their hair relaxed. But no.

I remember writing my feelings on the subject on paper when I was young.

My mother just doesn't understand; she always has to play the strict-mom card, like she would be less of a mother if she loosens up a bit. Or, if she does anything different from what her siblings are doing with their kids, or how her mom handled all of them, or how my great-grandmother brought up her kids. To sway from those patterns would be as if she broke some unspoken law. She doesn't understand the pressure of growing up today. It's bad enough that almost all my girlfriends have had their periods and I have to listen to their complaints about period cramps. I'm second to last to get it, and on top of that, I have to walk around with this colitas in my hair too like I'm five years old. I even hear the girls talking about boyfriends.

Looking back, I think boys are one of the reasons my mom wouldn't let me relax my hair. I always told her that she acts like she never had a childhood, to which she'd always respond, "It's because I did that I'm this way with you."

In the Dominican Republic (D.R.), once a female starts

showing a flourished body figure, men start lining up, throwing lustful looks, letting the women know they're in line. They assume you ought to feel flattered because they're interested in you. Eventually, you'd have to assist them in their request to be with you, or at least that's what they expect. But getting your hair relaxed is the ultimate sign that lets them know you've become a woman who's ready to date. And your ever-developing body is their green light. You don't get to say no because your body and relaxed hair are saying yes. This coming of age moment for a girl is the norm, introduced to you from a young age. You have no further knowledge or anything else to compare it with, so you simply take it in the same way you would take in the ocean-kissed breeze.

Curly hair was the most prominent hair type I saw growing up, including my own. Yet, it was and still is the most hated and least appreciated hair type. The irony. But, like some illness or disease, we're told there is a treatment for it. The chemicals to straighten hair come in a box that's littered with disclaimers and warnings as if it were poisonous cleaning supplies and side effect-ridden medication.

First, you start by doing the piggy tails, sometimes braids, but letting it free is not an option unless you're swimming. Otherwise, you'd be walking around with un *pajon,* which everyone would make sure you know because you'd become the punch line of everyone's jokes. Then, when you felt too old for piggy tails, you'd have it relaxed. It was a win-win situation: easy-to-manage hair for mom, and you'd get a feel of womanhood. Relaxing your hair meant fitting in with the other girls and qualifying to be objectified by boys. I never saw it as a bad thing, but as a positive thing, because it meant I was checking all the boxes of beauty.

Growing up, you dream of your hair when its pattern is stretched out to the core, and its waves are no more, renouncing the lineage of different hair types in your family. We treated it as a calamity that we were so unlucky to inherit. But it wasn't just about having straight-relaxed hair. It was about all the extra effort that came with this mature look. I wanted to have hair that listened and was considered "good hair." Albeit, your life does become complicated with straight hair too, as I came to find. Now, you have to say goodbye to carefree swimming.

Otherwise, you'll be living at the hair salon. Funny thing is, relaxing my hair didn't come with any of the feelings I thought it would. There was no freedom. In fact, it felt more like a sentence. There was no boost in confidence. Really, it was just one more thing to be self-conscious about. But, it's all us Island Girls knew.

If I knew the ocean was going to be just a memory, and whatever I packed with me had to be enough for me to remember the place I grew up, I would have packed more. I would've swum deeper. I would have grabbed every ray of sunshine. I would've let my perfect pattern curls spend more in the hot sun. I would have appreciated how well my skin and the sun got along. I would have gorged on mangos from Papa Hombre's mango tree—or, honestly, from any neighborhood's house—until I was sick from the sweet-sour flesh.

Every day, I miss the non-stop waves outside my window. I had to travel across the sea to appreciate my Island-Girl life. I had to step out of the scene and watch it on the screen to know that I was truly living my best life on the island.

Now, in my new home, the only window view I get is

a trash can where my whole apartment building throws its waste and a corner store on the other side. This view is all I know of my new world now. My family and I just got here, and some girl came knocking on the door, accusing us of throwing a garbage bag from the fourth floor down to a large trash can—such a warm welcome. You know, Nueva York (aka New Jersey), you are not as great as the place I left behind.

It's fascinating how, when I was growing up, the things I considered ordinarily minor or didn't appreciate because they were just handed to me are now the things that I crave every day. This brings my emotions to the surface when I look around and contemplate this new reality. I miss the blooming Trinitaria tree at Mama Pula's house, showing off its beautiful, velvety petals. I used to love looking at it during the sunset. But then, come sunrise, Papa Hombre would make me sweep up all the fallen petals that fell like autumn leaves during the night. I never quite understood how it became my job. But, I did what I was told (unlike my cousins who said no to him) despite my childish loathing of doing it.

I think growing up witnessing the immensity of the

ocean and its gradients of blue waters that never get tired makes you grow up being a dreamer. I've always been a tiny girl, but sometimes my dreams feel bigger than the ocean. Dreams which seemed less impossible the moment I found out I was moving to the States and dreams that were crushed the moment I stepped outside the plane on a summer hottest day. *Viajeros* paint you a picture when they visit Santo Domingo from the United States, with their expensive outfits and the special treatments they get when they're there; this makes you wonder what kind of money-growing-on-trees paradise they are coming from. They do not mention the high rents and the never-ending cycle of living paycheck-to-paycheck. If people would at least be honest about living in the U.S., I'd have been mentally prepared for the hustle instead of thinking I was going to be greeted by a butler and welcomed into a castle.

AS MY MOM, TWIN SISTERS, PAULA AND PAMELA, and I approached the unfamiliar school building in this unknown new city, we were terrified by it. This school could be ten times bigger than any other school I have seen in my life, and my anxiety levels rise an enormous amount, enough to fill up the building. *"Hablas Español?"* my mom timidly asked a girl who was putting the school flag away. She stared at us but did not stop rolling the flag's rope around her left arm. She looked like she did not want to socialize with strangers, *but she had to,* I thought, because she spoke Spanish. We needed help finding a way to greet this vast school, which also didn't seem like it wanted to socialize with strangers. It turns out it was just her face because she ended up being the sweetest girl, and introduced all four of us to the school.

There are two types of Latin immigrants in the U.S., those who use their bilingualism to help Spanish-speaking people and others who put their Spanish away to avoid helping anyone who doesn't speak English.

We walked closer to one of the many school entrances and entered the empty halls. I remember the walls were covered in flyers for special events and sports tournaments. I wondered what superpower you had to have to be displayed on these walls.

The school was tranquil. Nearly everyone was out due to summer break. We were greeted by a lovely lady who brought us into an office where, despite its openness, it somehow still felt private. While walking us through a lot of paperwork, the school admissions lady asked, *"A que academia le gustaria pertenecer?"* My sisters turned to stare at me as if I knew what to say.

She explained that the school was divided into three academies: Culinary, Technology, and Government. But really, it didn't matter what we chose. We did not understand a thing.

I figured I was never good in the kitchen like my mom; I did not want to be cooking at school. Technology seemed hard and more well-suited for kids from the American movies that had above-average intelligence—those kids who can dream of attending Ivy League schools with big names and sky-high tuition costs. We were left with the Government Academy. This also meant we had to be part of the Junior Reserve Officers' Training Corps (JROTC). At that point, I didn't know what the JROTC was, but I thought I would probably be forced to join the U.S. Army eventually. Still, we went with those odds.

We finally finished the registration process at Eastside

High School, me as a Junior and my younger twin sisters as Sophomores, whatever that means. I thought as long as they didn't put us in a lower grade than we were supposed to be in, everything would be fine.

TO BE ENROLLED AT EASTSIDE HIGH-SCHOOL, MY SISTERS AND I needed to get vaccinated—easier said than done. There were many entire mornings and afternoons spent in fluorescent-lit waiting rooms, parsing through old magazines that I could look at. The scariest part was not knowing where to go or how to get there. We took long walks across the streets of Paterson. We walked to the wrong building. We walked the opposite way from where we needed to go. Until we learned to take the bus. Then, I'd be terrified of yelling "stop" when we needed to get off. It felt like Paterson was starting to like us because everywhere we went we found nice people who helped us with filling up the forms and answering the many questions the nurses had because each word felt like a puzzle… a puzzle with no color or imagery to follow.

When you come to America, you have no choice but to adapt. My family had no choice but to adjust. Me and my mother and sisters, but also my aunt, uncle, and cousins. Eleven of us, all living in the same two-bedroom apartment. It felt like a hot sancocho on a scorching day. But we made it work, even if Pam, Pau and my cousin, Julia had to sleep on the floor. I wondered, *is this legal?* I don't think it is, but I'm grateful to the landlord for allowing it.

During this time, my mom, aunt, and uncle were moving earth and sea to find jobs to pay rent. Thankfully, my mom's youngest sister, who had been living here for years, rented the apartment and paid for the first month. She's a Pastor, so maybe it's the Jesus in her that guides her generous heart.

While the adults were worried about jobs to cover rent and expenses, the kids had to start worrying about school. Summer was coming to an end, and I had no idea what to expect or how to prepare. My new school was different in every possible way from the one I had grown up in. I was overwhelmed by the thought. It wasn't just the language that terrified me, but also the people. *Would I blend in? Where do I start?* I was hoping that my lack of English would make me invisible to my classmates, that if I couldn't communicate, I would just blend into the background. Thankfully, it did.

Thankfully, our school was within walking distance of our apartment, and we were able to walk there every morning. Walking there that first day felt like walking to my execution. I had no idea what to expect, but my body was buzzing with nerves.

I entered the school with my sisters, terrified to be among the other students. It seemed as though everyone except us had a place within the school, and it was strange to feel so left out. It felt deeply odd to be at a place where you feel like everyone has a place in it but you.

We had to separate to go to our homerooms, and my nerves calmed when I realized homeroom was just a place to take attendance. I was glad to have a few more minutes to adjust to this new normal before the day truly began.

When the bell rang to signal our first class, I freaked out. All I had was a paper with many room numbers on it that I didn't know how to find. I had no idea where I was supposed to go. *"Necesitas ayuda con tu horario?"* a girl asked when she saw me.

"*Si, me puedes explicar por favor?*" I replied. She turned her school schedule into a map, explaining exactly where I should go and how to read my own schedule. She then ran to class to avoid being late.

I knew where I had to go, but I was still scared of all of the big hallways, the rooms, the lockers, the teachers, and especially the students. I was put in a bilingual class, and, for the time being, all of my classes would be in Spanish. *Lovely,* I thought. Maybe this would be okay after all.

But the dream quickly ended when, in my third period, the teacher didn't speak Spanish. I immediately felt the nerves come back to my body as I passed by the English-speaking students. A blonde curly-haired girl caught my attention. She isn't white, but she isn't black either. *Does she speak Spanish?* I wondered. I kept walking and found myself a seat in the back. As the teacher spoke, I watched the other student's notebooks fill up with words while my pages remained blank. After a while, the teacher approached me and looked down at me from over the top of his glasses, "Why are you not writing?"

he said.

I stared at him but had no answer to give. Another girl seated right next to me kindly translated, *"Por qué no estás escribiendo?"* I told her I don't speak English. She then told the teacher, and he turned away as if he didn't see me anymore. As he continued to dictate, she tried to write and translate for me at the same time. I knew she was struggling, but she was moving fast, and I was grateful for her efforts. Eventually, we realized this was not going to work, and she advised me to see my school counselor to switch classes. She helped me submit a form for the class change, and I hoped that the transfer would take place before I had to go back to that class again.

As I was leaving the class, the girl whose race I couldn't identify kept staring at me with her big brown eyes, her big curls bouncing off her shoulders. I stared back and said a quiet *"hola"* which she ignored and walked away. I watched her walk through the hallways. I assumed she didn't speak Spanish.

After a day passed, during my Spanish class, my counselor showed up to talk with me. He spoke for over a minute; I didn't interrupt to remind him I didn't understand English. I'm not American, but I know that interruptions are rude in every language. When he finished, I said, "no English." The phrase, which became a shield that I could hide behind and the door that got me out of any uncomfortable situation. The whole class stopped what they were doing to watch us. After an uncomfortable silence, my Spanish teacher translated what the counselor was saying. I was to be moved from my third-period class, English-speaking course into a culinary class. It wasn't what I wanted, but I was hoping it'd at least be better for me.

I didn't want to take culinary classes, but I knew I would rather be cutting vegetables than trying to write the words of a foreign language. The culinary class wasn't bad at all. I met other Dominican girls, Laura and Dayi and Jee, who was a funny black guy who always told me jokes as if I could understand him. We automatically became a little group, and both Laura and Dayi helped me get by in the class. We spent most of the time in the kitchen preparing sandwiches for the students' lunch. Once a week, we'd watch a video on a fat old T.V. on a high metal shelf that the teacher would roll out from another room. I tried watching the videos to gather information from the little I could understand. Jee, on the other hand, would always nap. Every week we would have a pop quiz about what the head chef taught us or about the video we watched. I grew more comfortable in class, eventually comfortable enough to study in advance of the quizzes. I felt like I'd found my crew. The chef would break us into groups to ask us questions about the quizzes. I admired how each student fought to give the right answers, and I envied their ability to do so. So, I continued to study hard. One day as I was telling Laura an answer to a question when a girl sitting behind me with big eyes that became even wider when she looked me right in the eyes and told me to be quiet because I did not know English.

I WAS ALWAYS TERRIFIED OF THE LUNCH PERIOD. I worried I would end up being like one of those girls in the movies, eating lunch alone in a bathroom stall. But lunchtime offered a break in the day, a chance to recharge, and I was thankful for that.

For lunch, we had a little card that allowed us to get our food and they would punch a hole on it each day.

The food looked great, definitely an upgrade from the small carton of milk and a tiny muffin like they served back home. At first, I just followed what everyone else was doing. I grabbed my food and followed the other students to the register, holding my lunch card in one hand, ready to be hole punched and my heart in the other hand. Everybody in front of me got their card hole punched; however, when it was my turn, the old lunch lady with gray hair and a nest on her head said something to me in English. Unable to understand her, my face folded with no clue of what to do next. I chose not to ignore her nor walk away. She repeated herself again, but with an attitude this time. *That won't make it any easier to understand you,* I thought. She followed by quickly snatching the lunch from my hands. Shocked at the scene, I shamefully walked to a table, hoping that no one else noticed. I tried to be strong, but couldn't hold back my tears, so I bowed my head down on the lunch table. After a few seconds, I felt a tap on my shoulder, and someone said, *"Estás bien, que te pasa?"* When I looked over my shoulder, it was the brown-eyed girl I'd noticed in class. She had my lunch in her hands and explained that, in addition to my lunch card, I needed to pay .50 cents. She then left to sit with her friends. Though I never really got to know her, I'd always think of her as a friendly face.

My last class of the day was also my shortest, and so I knew no matter what it'd be my favorite. The teacher was Puerto Rican and bald, a really cool person with an Argentinian accent that reminded me of Rebelde Way. His name was Mr. PJ. He taught History. I don't know why, but he always carried a large backpack with him everywhere. I thought he was probably the first person I'd encountered at school that didn't associate my lack of English with stupidity. Although his class was taught in Spanish, all the materials were written in English, a sort of forced-learning technique. His class was the most fun of them all, and I felt that with his help, I could be an outstanding student again.

Soon, my life became a routine, and I got used to my surroundings. The classes and faces were not so unfamiliar anymore. I met a lot of Hispanic kids having the same struggles as me. Though many of them still didn't speak English, they understood the school system and were able to get by. As the days passed by, I too became more familiar with the school, and it didn't scare me anymore.

Every day I'd go to school and come back home to watch Ana Doctora Polo's show, Caso Cerrado, with whoever was at home. The show always started with an inspirational quote, a way to soften the drama that the show always erupted into. And I should have a notebook somewhere filled with all of those life-fulfilling quotes. And so began my afternoons for the entire summer, fall, and winter. Saturdays became lazy days, and Sundays were, by default, church days.

After a while, I was being forced to Sunday service every week. I'd been in America for a year, and was wondering how long I'd have to put up with church. "We have to support my sister's church," said my devoted Christian mother. She's been a Christian her entire life; I think that is the first memory I have of her.

My mother didn't have enough money to spend on other things other than food and housing. I was only 14, so obviously, my mom's priorities were not my own. I never had anything to wear that fit my high fashion standards. I was angry with myself for having left so many clothes and belongings with friends in the D.R.. I would have been happier in church if I had clothes I felt good in, but we simply couldn't afford them.

I met a lot of friends at school and blended in with the other bilingual girls, some of whom were Dominican. We had a lot of classes together, and they made life better. I made a Facebook profile and added all my friends. I'd scroll through their photos looking at their pictures with the pretty clothes I wanted. Sometimes they would take pictures during lunch and post them. A lot of them are always posting "Something cute on your wall" or "like for a TBH" posts or whatnot. I found it annoying, but I always liked their posts because I wanted to know what they thought about me. I realized I wanted to be part of it. I know it shouldn't matter, but I was craving the validation I knew their attention would bring.

One day when I got home, I opened my Facebook account, and I saw that I was tagged in a photo. I got a little excited thinking maybe they did like me after all. However, I realized we'd never taken a photo together. It was a photo of me posted by Christina, a Dominican girl who formed part of the bilingual girls I sat with during lunch. I hated that photo, hated how it lowered by self-esteem even more. I cried as I read the comments, wanting to lash out at her the same way everyone else seemed to be lashing out at me. I then felt better about the whole thing and didn't have the need to ask her why or get revenge. Other friends in the group had other plans. They took a picture of her with half of an orange on her mouth. I wasn't mad at them for doing it and commented on the picture "haha" Christina, then replied, "como quiera Ela soy mas linda que tú", I then realized that this is not about me she's just an ugly person. I looked away and minded my business, *you don't waste your time with people like that,* and I never liked her again after that.

In fact, I had other problems. Real life problems. Like any high school junior, I was busy prepping for my senior year, carefully making sure I met all the requirements for college. I knew I'd have to take placement tests, and I knew I wasn't ready for them. I just got here, was my constant thought, but it didn't matter. I wanted everything to slow down and allow me to get ready for this new life. I started to wonder if maybe it'd be better to quit school and get a job. My head was spinning with possibilities.

My sisters, thankfully, were only sophomores and had an extra year to prepare for college. They're bright by default, decisive and intelligent in a way that's enviable. They seemed to be handling school well, which I was thankful for. The thought that they might be going through the same things as me made me panic. They don't know it, but they've always been my soft spot.

CHAPTER 2

NATIONAL HISTORY DAY

In History class with Mr. PJ, I learned so much about the United States. I learned that July 4th is Independence Day, and that many people celebrate it with fireworks. A few months into the course, Mr. PJ introduced us to the infamous National History Day competition. At a parent and teacher meet and greet, he said to my mom, "Your girls have the potential to make it to the finals, I know, I know..." He was much too close to her face, and smiling creepily at her. I honestly didn't think I could win, but I believed Mr. PJ had enough confidence for all of us, so we decided to go for it.

We started preparing for the competition that same week, doing research and determining what topic we'd like to present on. Mr. PJ decided we should study the three Mirabal sisters, and I was immediately hooked. He printed out a few articles for us to read. He didn't hand to us like a normal teacher would. He rolled up the black and white paper and hit us in the head with it.

I knew all about these heroic sisters; I did presentations and drawings of them when I was little. Every November, I participated in marches and protests for International Day for the Elimination of Violence Against Women. The day originated after the three sisters were ruthlessly assassinated by Trujillo's cruel regime. It's thrilling that I'll get to share a huge part of my culture with the U.S., but even more thrilling is to know that there are people interested to hear what I have to say about it.

I started thinking about the brave and fearless Minerva, Patria, and Maria Teresa. And, of course, the root of all evil, Leonidas Trujillo. I can proudly talk about our history, no problem; the issue is translating all this information in my head. So frustrating to know that this might take away from the story, and my limited vocabulary will not accurately portray the story and its message. It helps that I am doing it together with Pau and Pam.

Mr. PJ put together a big group of students and they all have a historic topic like us. I got to meet some incredible people. It was the most fun I had in high school so far, and the most I felt like I belonged. Every group presented on their own topic, and they were all very interesting.

One day, all the groups met after class to discuss their projects. That's when I met Star. She was a typical high school nerd, and a good friend of my sisters. I immediately found her annoying, mostly because she seemed like a know-it-all. I wish how I met one of my closest friends would be a different story where you get along and grow straight into sisterhood. Though I didn't know it at the time, she's the kind of girl that gets you in every way. Also, the kind of friend that surprises you with the yellow frame that matches Monica's apartment because she knows she's the one responsible for your *Friends* obsession.

As the days got closer to the competition day, I became more anxious and nervous. One week before the event, we were excused from all of our classes to work on the presentation. We got a 3-part 4ft wood board and covered it nicely with a gray material that would help the pictures and text stand out. We started printing out pictures and maps and important items that are crucial to the story. We tried including every detail that would make the presentation more impactful.

Each picture was cut carefully, mounted on foam, and placed on the wood board for a 3D effect. Each photo told a story, starting from the upper-left corner down to the bottom right corner. We added pictures of the beautiful island map and many old pictures as we found online. There were many pictures of Trullijo, clothed in a military outfit, holding meetings with other important leaders. We then followed with pictures of Minerva, Patria, and Maria Teresa. The butterflies, how they're also known. There were far fewer pictures of the sisters online than there were photos of Trujillo. But each picture found seemed to scream with heroism and courage, their message as loud as their impact on our country was profound.

I knew the entire history by heart by the day of the competition. By the time Trullijo elected himself as a candidate for the presidency of the Dominican Republic, the country was in the U.S. Army's hands. They supported Trujillo's election because of his background and high position in the Dominican National Guard, which was founded by the U.S.

Leonidas Trujillo gained his power by torturing and killing anyone who opposed his candidacy. As his power and fame continued to increase, the people grew to fear him. During his presidency, citizens were required to hang a picture of El Jefe at home, right next to a picture of Jesus. In other words, he wanted the people to pretend to believe that he second only to God. But, I'd say that he was the next best thing, yes, after Satan.

He championed the phrase "Dios y Trujillo," lighting the skies with a neon sign so the city could see. Even the Capital, Santo Domingo, he renamed after himself. Ciudad Trujillo. He renamed one of the Dominican's most visited cities, El Pico Duarte, after himself. *El Pico Trujillo*. He used restoration efforts after national disasters to remodel entire cities in his honor. He was reshaping the country, and the people all knew it. It was the beginning of the end of our democracy; of our voice. He intended to kick everyone out and keep the country for himself. His supercharged ego and immoral behavior didn't fit on the Island with everybody else. Especially Haitian immigrants, many of whom were also assassinated by the Trujillato with the intention of *"no dañar la raza."*

Yes, when he was in power, he brought the country's economy to a stable state. But what does any of it mean without freedom? What does it mean if people didn't feel safe in their own homes? When the people's properties, assets, and daughters were not off-limits to Trujillo's desires? When many people lost their lives, not only for rebelling against his regime but also for their skin color; what does it mean? I'll tell you what it means… It means war, and it all started with the many tries and failed attempts to end his dictatorship.

Las Mariposas, my heroes — the definition of intelligent, independent, fearless women. The Mirabal sisters showed their disapproval of the regime, and were motivated to join every group or clandestine activity against the dictatorship. The sisters revolutionized our country. They were incarcerated and tortured, again and again. But, they kept going. Until they became Trujillo's biggest threat. He planned and commanded the assassination of the sisters, Las Mariposas. This was the people's breaking point. Minerva, being the eldest sister and leader, decided to pursue a career in law, but the right to education was taken away from her by Trujillo when she rejected his sexual advances. Maria Teresa and Patria followed their sister's steps to end the Trujillato.

They made it their mission to end this regime, even with the knowledge that fighting against Trujillo was a death sentence. To which Minerva said, *"Si me matan, sacaré los brazos de la tumba y me haré más fuerte."* This translates to: *"If they kill me, I'll reach out my arms through my thumb, and I'll be stronger."*

Though they were born into the Trujillo regime, they did not accept it as normal. Instead, they risked their lives to improve the lives of generations to come. Even when it seemed that they wouldn't win, they continued to fight.

El Trujillato was a scary time. The walls could talk, the air you breathed told your secrets, traveling to the ears of Trujillo's soldiers telling stories like a newspaper. It's people like the Mirabal sisters that change everything. They leave their footprint on History, not just changing it but creating a story that we can trace back and be reminded that we are, in fact, capable of bringing about change when faced with injustice. They did not make it alive, but because of them, we did.

After we finished our presentation, we ran outside to meet Mr. PJ and the others. He told us that he was proud of us for just coming out. We then grabbed lunch and waited for the results.

National History Day was the most I'd seen of America altogether. I saw people of all races, ethnicities, and backgrounds. I had never seen so many races together in my entire life, and I was amazed by it.

The results were in. We were nervous and excited as we entered the auditorium, where everybody was waiting, wishing to be called up to the stage and told we'd be going on to the next round of the competition.

Finally, two people took the stage. "Thank you, everyone, for coming here," one of them said, channeling the enthusiasm of an awards show host. They announced the winners, giving each a blue ribbon. The kids who were announced walked excitedly across the stage, and everyone else remained seating, hoping their names would eventually be called. I knew that hearing my own name called would feel like a dream come true.

I loved our work, and our visuals were well done but with so many great presentations and smart, English-speaking kids to explain and present, I thought it was probably just a waste of my time. I highly doubted we would pass to the next round. The night before the competition, my sisters and I were stressed because we didn't have suitable outfits for this type of event. We thought our appearance would hinder us.

But, when they announced our names, "Rafaela, Paula, and Pamela" the entire group from EHS jumped out of their chairs and screamed. I was happy, mostly because I sincerely loved seeing my sisters win, and I was glad to share their joy. Everyone from our school had passed to the next round, which would take us all the way to Washington D.C.

The following Monday, we returned to school. The excitement from the previous week acted like a motivator, spurring us forward once again. We were given an outline with ways to improve our project for the state-level presentation. In the first round, we were representing EHS, but now we'd be representing all of New Jersey. We were all in a circle surrounding Mr. PJ as he read the critiques we received after the first round.

"Muy Importante." I saw it written on the back of the

sheets and circled in red. My sisters and I shook our heads, surprised to learn that one of our judges spoke Spanish. She also let us know that the following year, translators would be available to non-English speaking students because of our project; because of us. *Just by this, we have already won*, I thought to myself.

Although we had a week before Washington D.C., we were not allowed to fix or change anything on our presentation board, or we would be automatically disqualified. So, we got together to polish and practice our oral presentations.

THE DAY FINALLY COMES TO HEAD TO WASHINGTON D.C. The night before we left, my sisters and I planned our outfits, preparing for the three days we'd be away from home. The next morning, we went to Kennedy High School, which many of my peers say is second worst in Paterson, lagging only behind our school. Our own group met with the students from Kennedy and a few other neighboring schools. We had a pretty solid group, and were excited and happy just to have the experience. The students from Rosa Parks High School were lovely, and we quickly bonded, remaining close throughout the whole trip. We made a few stops for food, and my sisters and I always fell back on our safe order: chicken tenders and fries with a Sprite. Hard to beat that, really.

It was a very long trip, but we finally made it to College Park, Maryland. I had thought my school was big, I was wrong. Suddenly, EHS didn't seem so big anymore. College Park's campus was full of buildings and many students. I had never seen so many high school and college students together, and it honestly made me nervous. We were given key cards to open our dormitories (I found it fancy, being that I wasn't used to staying in dorms). We found our designated room, and settled in. After a while, we met with Mr. PJ back at the front desk.

We spent the rest of the day enjoying time with Mr. PJ. He made sure every day was a mix of school and fun activities. He carried his backpack with him everywhere, which we called his kidney which was always packed with necessities.

Early in the morning, Mr. PJ would meet us with a cup of coffee and a book in his hand and his kidney on his back. He'd do a headcount, make sure we were all there, and then let us get on with the day.

All the New Jersey students were getting along, and a group of girls came to my room to chat. They were African American, and despite the language barrier, they wanted to be friends with my sisters and me. I thought maybe it was because they knew what it was like to not fit in. For the first time since moving here, I finally didn't feel so alone. There were about ten girls together in a room, all high school students away from adults for the first time, and excited to get into some trouble. They ignored the 10:00 PM curfew, and though I'm not usually one to break the rules, I didn't care this time. I had friends, and that's all that mattered.

We broke into groups and started running through the hallways and down the stairs. I'm not sure of what we were playing, but I was following Rose, a short-haired, kind-hearted girl. The moment I saw her, I admired how well she rocked her hairstyle. So when she started running, I just followed her. We stopped by a room where some blonde, blue-eyed girls were, and Rose stopped to say hello.

"Do you need anything?" The girls were asking nicely, but I could tell by how uncomfortably close one was to Rose that they wanted us out.

"No, we are just playing", Rose replied.

"Oh, okay, where are you guys from?"

"We're from New York City," Rose said, smiling and making eye contact with me.

We're from Jersey. Why is Rose lying I wondered.

"Nice to meet you," the girl said. "Have you seen the students from New Jersey?"

"They're so weird. They scare me." another one of the girls with her added, covering her mouth with her hand while the other girls laughed.

Rose looked at me, and though she didn't say anything, I knew what she was thinking. *Welcome to America.*

"It was nice meeting you girls", Rose said in an odd voice, different from how she normally spoke.

We ran back to the room to join the other girls, and Rose seemed fine, as if the other girl's comment didn't bother her at all. But it was not normal to me, and I was confused as to why she wouldn't defend her friends. And what did this girl mean by weird?

We were the last to return, and everybody was seating

in the room. Rose started joking about what had just happened, telling everyone how stupid the girls were. Everyone started laughing; they were all very unbothered. It was the first real glimpse I had of just how much racism permeates American culture.

Eventually, we all went to sleep, but I knew I had trouble shaking what had happened. When I went to bed, I began to analyze and repeat the scene in my head, trying to find the weirdness in us that girl seemed to be so taken by. Some of my classmates came to mind, and even some of the things that we were doing earlier that day. We were, admittedly, a very diverse group of people. We laughed a lot and joked around. Could she have been referring to when we were playing volleyball earlier, and Juan, one of my classmates, wore skinny red jeans? Or how he was trying to do a flip? If that's what she meant by *weird*, I'm with her. He's my beautiful weirdo, though. But nothing else seemed weird or funny about us, I mean other than we were just human beings existing. I even questioned myself and what I was wearing. Unable to make sense of her words, I fall asleep, disappointed that someone would speak so cruelly without even really knowing us.

The morning after, we meet with Mr. PJ and his friends. It was the day we'd finally see everyone's presentation. From historical skits to technology and traditional exhibitions, I loved it all. The art and history all meshed together, and the exposure to college life showed me what was next for me after high school.

After the exhibition, we were free for the rest of the day, so we wandered around campus to meet more contestants. I loved the college dorm life. I thought maybe it would be my life after I graduated high school. The small room and bed, the key to my own little place, the big cafeteria with its strict hours. I knew I would enjoy that lifestyle. I knew I could get used to it.

We visited a stunning museum, where I got to see some of the first airplanes ever built. It was such a fascinating experience, and motivated me to keep moving forward in this country.

Our New Jersey group differed from many of the other students. We were different races and spoke different languages, and maybe some people even thought we were a little weird. Even still, everyone sought us out to say goodbye, collecting the state pins we brought along with us.

We didn't make it past the initial round, so we left D.C. earlier than we thought we would. By the time we left, I realized I had actually become very close with my sisters' friend, Star. I was glad I got to share the event with her. I got a taste of how the American college life would be like. It was too far ahead to think about, but I wanted it. I was ready to spend my hours studying to pass whatever tests I needed to pass to get the key to open the door to my next adventure.

After Washington, I returned to school with a new mindset and wonderful new friends. I knew my senior year would be stressful; I was still catching up on credits from the previous year. However, it was okay that my journey didn't look like everyone else's, or that most of my friends were headed to college. I knew it'd be taking the entrance exams, too, but the thought of passing them was keeping me up at night.

My first year at this school took a whole lot of adjusting to the new people, the new environment, and life in general. It had been a year since I'd moved to Jersey, and the language forced itself down my throat. I was familiar with it, maybe not to speak it fearlessly, but to understand what others were saying when they spoke or wrote. I knew just enough to sit across from my mom at our dining table while she attentively waits for me to translate her mail in full Spanish which I was partially understanding in English. I learned to cope, to walk through life silently, hoping I could get away with small talk and not have to have in-depth conversations with anyone. It made me seem unfriendly, but it was the best I could do at the time.

Junior year was unlike any other in my life. I developed an enormous fear of social interactions, coping with the days one at a time while having no idea of what to do next. I discovered new feelings and emotions, many of which seemed to have been waiting to burst out of me for years. As my social interactions with humans decreased, my interaction with paper and pen increased. I've always worried about the future, so most of my brain space was occupied with the unknown. Writing things down was the only way I knew to process life sometimes.

I often was concerned about how we carried ourselves

through life, knowing we were going to die someday. Why weren't we doing bigger things? Why weren't we trying to achieve the things we always hoped, thriving to make the world a better place for those who are here and those who will come? I felt that I needed to move through my journey alone, because no one else seemed to care. My cousins were too busy trying to save up to buy the next iPhone or outfit, or figuring out how to hide the next tattoo from their mom or how to sneak out of the house to the next party. I was never built like the typical teenage girl. I was an old soul. My cousin Julia was always looking for ways to be a rebel, and I walked in the opposite direction. I thought maybe that was why our friendship didn't survive. Despite being cousins and seeing so much of each other, we were too different to truly be friends after we were older. The last time I had hung out with her and her friends, I left early, crossing a railroad alone to get back home. They were going to her friend's house to meet with some boys, and I just wasn't down for that. Mostly, I was running because I was afraid none of them would be interested in me. I carried my worries around every day, like a backpack strapped full of books and notes that I could never catch up on.

My thoughts were interrupted by a phone notification. I reached to my front pocket to see what it was. As we passed the corner store a block away from the school where they sold the most greasey empanadas, Pau and Pam stopped to go into the store to get one. While I waited outside the store, I slid a finger across the screen of my phone and saw a text message from an unknown number. The text comes in blue so, I knew it was from an iPhone user.

iPhone user: Hi, I really loved your presentation on NHD, I wish I was that smart.

Me: Who are you?

iPhone user: This is Geovanny from Mr. PJ's class, I always see you with your sisters

Me: How did you get my number?

iPhone user: I asked your sisters because I see them in my other class

Me: Okay, well, thank you.

As we continued our way to school, my sisters were stuffing her face with their empanada, placing a left hand under their chin to ensure nothing fell on her school uniform. It's scary how identical my twin sisters were both in personality and appearance. My sisters were walking right behind me, but I didn't tell them about the boy who texted me. The thought of being noticed by someone who went through the trouble of getting my number just to tell me that he liked our presentation made me smile. It was like a weight had been lifted, or like a little hole had opened for me to move into and be more accepted by my peers. For the rest of the walk, I didn't mind any of the old and clumped together houses; they seemed more pleasant to look at. I was never so excited to walk to school.

CHAPTER 3

SENIOR YEAR

Senior year was looking rather wild for me. The majority of my friends had decided to go to Kean University, at Union City, NJ. Many of them told me that Kean was just a bus and a train away from our town, and I could still live at home. But anything further than a dollar bus ride away felt like thousands of miles from my mom and sisters. Julia, my cousin didn't end up going to college. She had a boyfriend, and he had helped her find a job. I wanted to follow my older cousin's steps, giving up on education and instead just getting a good job that paid well. It seemed like the most logical option. But my dreams allowed me to look even further ahead in the future. So far ahead that I couldn't make the drastic choice of not going to school.

I told my mother about college; she insisted I go for it, saying that she knew I could do it, and that I had her support. There's not been a day in my life, even now, when my mother's support hasn't covered me like a blanket over my shoulders, wrapped around my arms pressing against my chest.

Realistically though, I didn't have a job, and I didn't want to add another item to my mother's long list of bills. Besides, it seemed silly to put in so much effort when I knew I didn't meet the admissions requirements. But I needed to make moves; that much I knew. I worked with my school counselor to start the application process. I made an appointment to meet with him after school; it was torture going to his office. The walls and narrow halls that once terrified me now seemed more like a refuge, keeping me safe from the life changes to come.

I approached the office, and was able to look through the small glass window on the door to see if Mr. James was alone and able to speak with me. He saw me, and from his chair, waved me into his office. While he proceeded to talk and walk me through the process, I started to browse around for unfinished thoughts in my head to keep me occupied. I wished I had been assigned a different person, someone I could really talk to. Instead, I was assigned a gray-haired man who had no understanding of my frustrations with the school, the exams, or life in general. He was solely there to do his job. What does he know about the struggles of a girl lost in a new country that promised her nothing but life greatness? I took my phone out to kill time and saw that I missed a text from *iPhone User* saying hello. Suddenly, my counselor visit didn't seem as bad. I was excited. "Hi", I instantly typed on my phone. But I didn't hit send right away. Instead, I decided to wait five minutes so I didn't look desperate. I kept looking at the clock on the wall, watching as the minute hand slowly made its way around the face. A minute passed, two minutes. I couldn't take it anymore, and finally hit send.

I had him saved on my phone as G, mostly just be-cause I didn't want my family to see a boy's name on my phone when they made their calls back to the Dominican Republic. I don't text that often, but G kept the conver-sation going, asking questions and genuinely trying to get to know me. I told him I was still at school with my counselor, but I was excited to leave so I could focus only on him.

A printer across the room started grinding while spitting out some paper, and by pressing down his arms again on the black office chair to lift up the rest of his body, Mr. James gets up and grabbed a stapler to glue multiple pages together and handed it to me and said, "here's everything you need to apply and let me know if you have any questions."

"Thank you," I said, leafing through the pages as I made my way to the door to leave. Immediately, I noticed I had an appointment scheduled with Kean University but had no recollection of agreeing to it. But before I had time to stress about it, I noticed G standing up against the wall outside Mr. James' office and knew right away he was waiting for me.

"Hey, I was in practice, and I wanted to know if you wanted to hang out." I stopped dead in my tracks, embarrassed that I couldn't find the right words to say in the right language. Eventually, I was able to agree, and we made our way to the school's exit, moving along with a strange but comfortable silence between us. I was able to text him anything, but right then I couldn't even bring myself to ask him where we were going. "Do you have a dollar?" He casually asked.

The silence between us is filled with question marks

floating in the air. "Yes?" I hesitantly replied while taking the dollar out of my backpack. I sorted my money, handing him a single bill which he grabbed without saying anything else. I didn't feel unsafe with him; he was a classmate after all. But I was entirely unsure of where this day was heading.

As we walked away from the school, I fished my phone out of my pocket to let my mom know I might be late. I'd been hanging out with the kids from National History Day after school a lot, so I let her assume that's what I was doing. While looking at my phone screen, G's voice reached my ears, asking me who I was texting. I took my attention from the screen and looked at him, and replied, "my mother." When G and I approached the bus stop, still, not a bone in my body was brave enough to question him. While we waited for the bus, neither of us said a word, and I was starting to feel a bit awkward.

A dollar bus was approaching us, so G got up to get on, and I followed along. We continued to sit in silence, but he sneakily grabbed my hand, and I felt all the feelings, I felt my heart up in my throat. That went on for about twenty-five minutes. He was holding my dollar, and pulled another one out of his shorts. I looked around, realizing he was preparing to get off the bus. I recognized the neighborhood. We weren't that far from school, but were far enough that I knew the neighborhood was nicer and safer than my own.

"Next stop", G yelled to the driver while pulling me off the bus. There was something about someone pulling me by my arm while walking in front of me that made me feel nervously good about this moment. I felt wanted and cared for.

I noticed the sidewalks in this neighborhood were cleaner than my home, and I saw fewer and fewer corner stores. After the bus took off, G let go of my hand and started walking. He was a few feet ahead of me when he turned and asked, "How was your day?" I tried to act normal, as if someone asking about my day wasn't a rarity, especially coming from a Mexican-American boy who just so happened to be in a bilingual class with us.

Unable to say anything else, I said, "Okay." We walked by the houses, all divided by a driveway between them, big enough to build another house on. After a few blocks, we made a right and then left. Finally, he approached a two-floor house. We had to go up about ten stairs to get to the front door. He inserted the keys into the lock, and I couldn't help but feel anxious about what or who was behind the door. I'd never been allowed to bring someone to my house without announcing it first. It made me wonder if his parents were just really cool, or maybe not even home at all. If I had known we were heading to his house when he asked me to hang out, I probably would have said no. I hardly knew him, and it seemed like it could become an uncomfortable situation. But I didn't want to interrupt our moment or ruin his budding interest in me. So I stayed quiet.

When we entered the house, I noticed the front door opened into a small room attached to the house, the next door was made of glass from the middle part up, and I could see flashing lights as if someone was watching TV. Entering his house, I wasn't able to see all the rooms of the house at one glance. Everything was expanded to its pertained space.

We walked into the living room, big enough to fit two large couches and a 72" flat screen TV with space to spare. We made our way to the dining room, the table in the center so large I knew it would easily fit G's entire family. My eyes go far enough to see a hallway surrounded by closed doors on both sides. These are extra bedrooms, and the hallway seems to lead to the kitchen. His house was nice. I couldn't help but think that we might someday live in a house like this.

G signaled for me to wait and yelled out, "I'm home!" He walked towards the hallway, and I could hear whispering, and then steps approaching the living room where I was waiting. "Hola," said G's mom when she made it to the living room. She was smiling sweetly, and introduced herself. Conversation seemed to flow easily with her, even though we were still strangers. I could tell she was studying me, silently pricing what I was wearing. The ripped jeans, my backpack, my Payless pink-plaid shoes. She continued to ask questions, making a real effort to get to know me. She didn't seem bothered by my presence, and I wondered if she was happy G had finally brought a girl home, or if she was just used to him always having a girlfriend around. G joined us after a while, just watching the conversation pass back and forth between his mom and me. I hoped I was making a good impression.

Suddenly, G pulled me away from his mother without even letting her finish her sentence. "Mucho gusto," I said over my shoulder to his mother as G opened his bedroom door. His room was freshly cleaned. He had his own bed, his own nightstands, his own TV, his own closet, and his own dresser. I leaned against the dresser, too shy to make eye contact. Suddenly, G got close to me, held my face in his hands and kissed me. I kissed him back, settling in to let him take the lead. Maybe, I thought, maybe, I should, and I deserved to feel this way without any guilt or shame.

When he said earlier he wanted to hang out, I had guessed I was going to be eating greasy empanadas somewhere by the school. Or maybe he would walk me home just to make sure I made it there safely. Whatever I thought was going to happen, I wasn't expecting this.

G took a few steps back without breaking away from me. He threw himself on the bed, dragging me down with him so I was lying on top of him. I was suddenly aware that his mom was just a hallway away, and that my mother didn't know exactly where I was. I don't think anybody had ever kissed me so intensely before. I was just there, lying on him, thankful that I didn't have to use words to try to express my feelings for him.

His hands were gently caressing my shoulders, but without warning, they were reaching into my jeans, exploring places I didn't say he was allowed yet. I quickly stopped him and got up. I sat on his bed, as disoriented as someone who had just woken up from a bad dream. He just laid there, covering his eyes with his arm. "I have to go," I told him softly. I worried he would hear the weakness in my voice and know he could convince me to stay. I hoped he wouldn't. I needed to leave. He got up and walked towards the door. I followed him, all the way back through the house and to the bus stop in silence. The silence was different this time, no longer filled with intrigue and hope, but with doubt and disbelief.

I stared at his back as he walked toward his house. I stood alone at the bus stop, hoping that one would come by soon.

I felt responsible for everything that happened between me and G. I knew I shouldn't have left school with him in the first place, and it was my fault for going along with it anyway.

I checked my phone the whole bus ride home, desperately hoping G would text me. I felt like whatever happened next was for him to decide. Finally, a text came through. He sent a link to a song, a heart emoji, and one simple message. "I'm sorry".

CHAPTER 4

THE BOOK CLUB

Every once in a while, I get a really good night of sleep. I'm not a morning person, and I don't intend to be one. Sometimes I even doubt that I'm a person at all. I wake up ten minutes before having to start walking to school, and that leaves me with about five minutes to hop into the shower, another five to find my uniform, put it on, and make a feeble effort at getting my hair done. My sisters try to wake me up several times in the morning, but I pay them no mind.

But, lately, the one thing that makes my eyes open in the morning, far earlier than normal, is a good morning text from G. Every morning I reach under my pillow to grab my phone and check for his text. I tap my phone screen to unlock it.

G: Good morning! I have to see you today

The one thing better than a good sleep is knowing that I am his first thought in the morning. It gives me the energy I need to happily get out of my own head and survive the day. We have been texting constantly for the past few days, but don't interact much in school. Other than some flirty looks when we run into each other, I don't talk to him, or he doesn't talk to me. Still, I'm satisfied with where things are right now. I still feel shy around him, and don't always know what to say or how to act, so this arrangement feels comfortable for me.

As I'm lying in bed, I type out my reply to G.

Me: Yes, I'll see you around at school. Come to my book club after school so you can meet my friends.

G: No, I want to spend time with you. I miss you

Me: Sorry, I have to go to book club, so today doesn't work.

G: Bet, okay, you don't want to see me?

I paused for a moment before I responded, not wanting to say the wrong thing. But I noticed the time and realized I only had five minutes to get ready before I had to leave. I only had time to find my uniform and get dressed. The twins were furious at me because I was making them late for school. We powerwalked the whole way, and I could feel their frustration as we passed the corner store where they usually stop for an empanada.

But they should be thanking me. I'm saving them money.

SINCE JULIA AND I HAVE THE SAME GYM CLASS, we always meet by the locker room door so we can change into our gym clothes together. As a crowd of students tried to jam through the doorway, I saw her arm reach out for me.

I don't always shave my legs during the winter, so I would often wear sweatpants during gym to hide my legs. At times, I'd even go so far as to put my sweatpants on right over my uniform khakis so I wouldn't have to change in front of the other girls.

Julia and I changed and joined the rest of the class in the gym. While playing and joking around with my friends, I could feel someone's eyes on me. I looked around the gym, my eyes eventually landing on G, right there in the same gym class. Suddenly, I was aware of my appearance; of the fact that I didn't have time to get ready that morning, and I was insecure about how I looked. I always am effortlessly, but today I'm more insecure than ever and I'm so aware of it. I felt conscious about everything I was doing, and was trying hard to act normal and hide my excitement of seeing him. I let my eyes go in the direction of his eyes, and when they did, we both smiled.

After class, Julia and I ran to the locker room to change before anybody else, moving quickly so we wouldn't be late for our next class. I was jumping on one leg, trying to remove my sweatpants without taking off my shoes. It was a fiasco, really, and in the middle of it all, I got a text from G.

G: Where do you guys meet

G: For your book club

Me: At the school library downstairs.

I was nervous he might actually come, aware that I still didn't always know how to act in front of him. Admittedly, I only invited him because I didn't think he would show, but I knew an afternoon at the book club would be less nerve-racking than a trip to his house.

I finished changing while waiting for a reply. I spend the rest of the day playing out scenes in which I could embarrass myself in front of G. I knew I should warn the other members of the book club that a boy might be coming, so I texted Star.

When I got to the library, Star was already there, her

face buried in the pages. She was the one who suggested the book we were reading, and was adamant about making sure everyone read at the same pace.

I've always loved being in the library. It's freeing, healing, and it allows me to travel to many different worlds of fictional and even those worlds and spaces that were before me. Even if the library didn't always carry the books I wanted to read, my heart still found a sense of belonging there.

I sat down and took my book out of my backpack while we waited for everyone else. I was anxiously waiting to see G.

When everyone arrived and took a seat, we started our discussion, talking about what we liked and didn't like about the book. I was laughing at something someone else had said when I noticed G standing by the door. I gave Star a look that told her he was here, and he was the one I was waiting for. My laughter transforms into a strange but good feeling that takes over my body. As he continued to walk toward our table, my heart raced a little faster. The feeling grew as he walked toward our table, but he passed by me and joined a girl sitting alone instead.

I was embarrassed so much, that it felt like the embarrassment trespassed the layers of my skin and showed on me like an extra layer of clothes that everyone could see.

"Where are you, seniors going for college?" Star asked. I knew she was hoping to give me a moment to compose myself, and I loved her for it. I smiled at Star, hiding my embarrassment and confusion and trying to act natural. I told her about my appointment at Kean University. It was a welcomed distraction, but I couldn't help staring across the room at G and the girl he was sitting with. They made sense. She was pretty. She could speak full and complete sentences effortlessly without stuttering any words. I couldn't hear what they were chatting about, but I could tell she was comfortable with him. I couldn't help but notice how she seemed to have everything I thought I lacked. It made sense, at that moment, why G would choose her over me.

That afternoon, after I got home, I laid in bed for a while, trying to process my emotions. Something I've never been good at. I felt betrayed and lied to. I needed some time to recover, so I shut my phone off and picked up a book, letting myself get deep into a world other than my own.

I laid flat on my bed, while my two hands hold down my head, and my eyes follow the perfect pattern of a well-formatted novel. I read a chapter that described abuse as what it is; abuse. It was portrayed in a foreign way to me, where the abuser is held accountable for their actions and part in the event and where the victim isn't blamed. The main character described how a family member had sexually abused her, and did so multiple times. It was almost too graphic, and I could feel tears of frustration welling in my eyes, my vision becoming blurred while images from my own life flashed through my head. Tears, but different and profound tears come down my eyes. Tears that waited decades to flow and help mourn something they knew I lost. I was amazed at the character's conviction, how she identified so wholly as a victim. She knew where she stood; knew that she had been taken advantage of in the worst way, but that none of it was her fault. I bet she never asked herself why she didn't make healthier choices. She knew that she didn't offer up her innocence. It was undeniably

and abruptly snatched from her hands. I deeply gasped,
I felt as if I had used all the oxygen left on my body in
the course of three seconds, it all gathered in my chest,
making me feel light and tight inside. I did not want to
release it because doing so would mean I had to admit I
was too a victim. I held my breath, waiting to let go until
I felt centered in reality again. Eventually, I let it all out
slowly and quietly, not wanting anyone to hear me. All of
me.

I worried that I'd never be the same, or that my rela-
tionships would never be the same. It was like relearning
myself. I put the book down and saw six messages from
G. It was clear he wanted to talk to me, despite what had
happened earlier.

G: Hi, how was your day?

G: Why are you so smart?

G: Really? Kay then

G: I'm sorry I showed up, she's just a friend

G: ?

G: Listen, I felt intimidated by your friends, and I
didn't know what to do

Me: Sorry, I was reading.

G: Are you mad at me? Can I see you tomorrow?

Me: I'm a little hurt because of what you did. No, tomorrow isn't a good day.

G: When can I see you?

Me: G, this is my last year, and I'm doing a lot. I don't think this is going to work out. Maybe we should just be friends.

G: Come on, give me a chance, I want to be there for you and help you through your senior year

Be there for me? I felt desperate. I wanted those words to be true.

Me: You're the sweetest.

While G's attention felt nice, I needed to focus on making it through high school so I could get into college. Even though I didn't want to pursue anything with G because of that, I couldn't resist the idea of having him in my life. I'd love for him to be there at my graduation. Maybe he would bring me flowers, and I'd feel special. I crave the idea of being with someone so much that I decided to just go with the flow.

THE WEEKS THAT FOLLOWED WERE HEC-TIC. AFTER VISITING KU, I started to wonder if college was really going to happen for me. The admissions costs were high, and the staff didn't seem as excited about my enrollment as I'd hoped. Even still, I had applied. I had given it my best effort, and now all I could do was hope they'd take me.

I have to say, it felt silly applying to college when I didn't even know if I would graduate high school. I was exhausted.

It was just too much. I found myself daydreaming more and more about life on the island. I was thinking about laying on a beach in the Dominican Republic when I should have been thinking about class work. Instead, I should have studied to pass the state exams that determine if I'd graduate.

THE STATE EXAMS WERE DIFFICULT, ONE OF THE WORST experiences I could picture. I felt like I'd failed already just looking at the test paper. We had open-ended questions. Most students hate this type of question by default, and I'm sitting there not fully comprehending what was being asked or the solution to the problem. It didn't matter how many times I read it, I couldn't make sense of any of it. The more I reviewed it, the more foreign it became. Nevertheless, I filled each one with fragments and grammar errors enough to drive whoever was grading this insane.

Each day that I had to take a test was just draining and hopeless. Math was a bit less wordy, not entirely. I saw people turning in their exams while I was still working through mine. The teacher is sitting facing us and probably fully aware of who will or will not pass. I forced myself to take my focus off of everything and put it on myself. On passing these tests. I re-read each question with a clear mind, freeing my mind from any other thoughts and allowing my brain to just, for now, pay attention to the words.

CHAPTER 5

SMALL TOWN

Los Patos is a beautiful town, located in the southern part of the Domincan Republic. Everybody knows everybody. On the Island, people seem to age in patterns, with every age group following their own prescribed norms. The adults, my parents and grandparents and aunts and uncles, they parented us all. They kept a watchful eye on us all the time and seemed to always be talking with each other, always aware of what we might be up to. Then there's the twenty-somethings, the ones we looked up to most. They always seemed to have it together, dating and voting and heading into the city for school. Those who made it out without getting pregnant were treated like royalty; they were the outliers.

And then there was me; my friends; the teenagers. We were always trying to do things we weren't supposed to, wearing makeup behind our mother's backs, or making out with boys when the sun went down. We used to roll up notebook paper and smoke it like cigarettes, laughing when we were able to blow a ring.

I started to test out my luck by slowly doing things I was not allowed to, trying to see if I could sneak it by my mother. I remember the day I tried to wear makeup in public. I was no older than ten, only brave enough to wear a single blue line of glitter under my eyes. But my mom noticed it as soon as she saw me, and it was clear from the look on her face that she didn't approve. I've gone too far. For my mom, this was as if I put on 100 layers of makeup, down to the foundation all the way to contour and passion-I'm-a-grown-up-woman red. She sent me back home to take it off. I can still see my cousin's face laughing at me as I walked away… the jerk. When I got home, I shaved off half my eyebrow after removing the eyeliner. I didn't like my eyebrows, and at that moment, I needed to do something drastic. Of course, my mom didn't approve of that either, but can you blame me?

It was common for young girls to run away with their boyfriends. Often it was because they got pregnant, but sometimes they were just tired of their parents. The majority would end up dropping out of school, living with their boyfriend's families and getting beat up by their partners.

I was very young when my cousin Tati ran away with her boyfriend to a nearby town. My mother and my aunt Eli, Julia's mother, went after her when they found out Tati's partner had been physically abusing her. I remember thinking they were some of the strongest, bravest women I knew. I went with them the day they went to bring her home, walking through the cemetery that divided our towns. We got to their house, a cute place, but it was old, the weathered wood painted a sky blue. When Tati opened the door, she had a black eye. The bruises all over the rest of her body stood out, a stark contrast against her fair skin.

We all sat down in the living room, me and my mom, Tati and my aunt, and Tati's boyfriend, even. My mom lectured them, trying to get Tati to understand that this didn't have to be her life. But when Tati looked at me, her eyes full of shame and guilt and regret, I didn't understand but I knew she would stay. There was nothing more we could do for her, so the three of us walked back home.

I like to think a lot of the decisions my mother made were to protect my sisters and me from such scenarios with a man. I know that a lot of her energy went into raising us so that we would never be in a bad position, never have to break through a window at 2:00 AM to get ourselves out of trouble. I know that each time she doesn't let me go to parties, ride on motorcycles, or take trips to other towns with my friends. She was always just trying to protect me.

I was only allowed to have sleepovers at my cousin Julia's house because she was family, but never at my friends'. I think she always knew that teenagers do the opposite of what they say they're doing. And she was right. But, despite everything, she started to trust me as I grew older, and I loved how our relationship was growing.

It's an age-old tale, boyfriends impregnating their girlfriends and then leaving them behind. The shame always fell on the woman; no one ever seemed to care about the man who left her this way. They just got to walk away, but that's never been true for a woman.

I WAS LUCKY TO LIVE NEAR EVERYONE I

LOVED. I lived within walking distance of everyone I knew and loved, with everything I cared for or also needed in my neighborhood. I went swimming in the river with my friends every day, and, when I was lucky, my cousins would take me to the ocean. But the river was my happy place. Although the water was as cold as snow, the sun kept us warm while we swam. We hung out there nearly every day after school. It was even the place we went if our house didn't have running water. Sometimes—my least favorite days—Julia and I would have to carry gallons of water from the river to our house so we could have water at home to drink and cook.

Papa Hombre, my dad's father always kept treats at his house, so we'd go there often. He had a mango tree, and his was the best in town. He sold them at Mama Paula's restaurant on the main street of the town. He had all sorts of fruits in his backyard, and I even had my very own cherry tree. Papa Hombre treated me like a princess. When I was young, he brought a young girl from Haiti to live with him and my grandma. I remember meeting her, thinking she and I might eventually be friends. But she made fun of my slim, boney figure. It took me a while, after that, to really warm up to her.

I remember a time I stayed for dinner at Papa Hombre's house, and I was given a nice plate, while sitting on the couch and holding the plate on my lab, I enjoyed the dinner Didi made for us. She then fixes herself a plate and joined me on the couch. Papa Hombre promptly told her not to sit on the couch when she was eating. I also got up because I didn't want to get in trouble, but he told me it was okay. I didn't enjoy the food anymore because I didn't like the taste of the feeling of being treated differently than a person I considered a family member. I didn't say anything because calling out your elderly is a serious crime in D.R. I went ahead and sat with her in the kitchen. It was then I encountered how normalized the racial discrimination against Haitians was among us.

EVERY SEMANA SANTA, *SPRING BREAK,* PEOPLE CAME FROM out of town. It was a nice opportunity to see people I hadn't seen in a while. Us women would braid our hair, and decorate the braids with colored beads. It was a long process, but I was always thankful to have my curls tamed for the duration of the week.

During Spring Break, the beach would be packed with new faces. There were so many tourists that didn't know how to swim, and drownings happened nearly every year. Eventually, they prohibited swimming in the ocean during the celebrations. Mama Pula would open up her little restaurant at the beach, and almost my whole family would hang around. The other restaurants were expensive, and mostly only frequented by tourists. I ate for free at my grandma's, though, as long as I helped out from time to time. A volleyball court would go up on the beach, and the adults would play intense games for hours. It was so much fun to watch. Everyone was skilled and athletic, so the games were exciting.

The week of Semana Santa was chaos, with constant swimming and chatting and generally being together. By holy Friday, my face had peeled different layers of skin. My body received more sun exposure than it could handle. But Monday, the beach was nothing but peace. Calm, after a week-long storm.

Mama Pula's house was everyone's favorite place. She was, quite simply, the best cook. In the Dominican Republic, many houses have two kitchens. The nicer one is always attached to the main house, but no one is ever allowed to use it. It's kept pristine, almost as if it's only really there for show. Then there's the less fancy kitchen; it's often older, in need of a little paint, with constant messes and a familiar kind of chaos that never seems to fade. Mama Pula's house was no exception. Her everyday kitchen is located all the way at the back of her property, past the restaurant and the main house, through the garden, in its own little structure in the yard. It's not in bad shape, that kitchen, but its years of use are evident. When you walk through the door, you can see in the scratched counters and dented stove that generations of women have been using this kitchen to serve delicious meals to their families.

Mama Pula's little restaurant had an open-door policy for the family; we were always welcome to eat there. She was the best host, so we, unsurprisingly, spent a lot of our time there. We always felt welcomed when we entered, and always left feeling calm and well-fed. The restaurant was in front of her home, painted in pink and white with figures made out of figs. She had *maracas* and *tamboras* and tiny little horse statues, mementos from her life on every surface she could find. She had wooden tables, painted pink. One day, an Italian man was visiting, he painted a picture with lots of fruits on the wall and wrote *"Da Pula, se comida bien."* This became the main decor of the restaurant since I remember.

I remember walking through her house to get to the kitchen in the back, and having to pass by her portrait of the Mona Lisa in her living room. We used to be scared of that painting, of the way her eyes seemed to follow you through a room. But, of course, we couldn't say anything about it to Mama Pula.

Behind the old kitchen was a cherry tree, and this tree just needed to have my name on it. Just like the one at Papa Hombre's house, I felt connected to that tree; I felt like it was mine. I would eat all the *cerezas*, and, the more I ate, the more *cerezas* would grow to feed me.

On the other side of the kitchen, Mama Pula had a lemon tree, and no one was allowed to even look at it without her permission. It was her sacred tree, and everyone knew it. But she also had a guava tree between the main house and the restaurant, and we'd often stop on our way out to eat right from the tree. Mama Pula's home was a giving sort of place, and we all loved it as such.

Truck drivers, travelers, and tourists visited Mama's Pula restaurant often, and as soon as a guest walked in, she greeted them. She didn't have a menu or anything, and instead would just tell her guests what she had cooked that day. You eat what she makes, take it or leave it. People always stayed, excited for a real taste of Dominican home-cooking. If it was a larger party, everyone hanging out in the back kitchen would help feed the guests.

Mama Pula had beautiful silverware and plates that she only used for the restaurant. They were stacked in the vitrine in the main house, so we'd have to make several trips for every service, carrying the plates out and back more times than I could count. My job was to set the tables and deliver food. I loved serving, mostly because I got to talk to so many people. When I needed a break, I'd hang out in the back kitchen, but never for very long. I was happy to help Mama Pula. She gave us so much, it felt good to help her in return.

One day I was sweeping the patio under the trinitarian tree, trying to figure out how I could make less work for myself. I wasn't being supervised that day, and after a while, I started wondering where everyone was. I walked through the restaurant and saw one of my older cousins—one of the ones I was allowed to go to the ocean with because my parents knew he would protect me. He was looking at me, almost as if he was waiting for me. Suddenly, without warning, he flashed me. I was stunned, shocked, glued to my spot. He nodded his head at me, as if we were apart of some kind of agreement. He must have walked away, but I honestly don't remember. I was too dazed to process it all. Next thing, we're sitting in the living room, alone again… is it the same day? I'm sorry, I don't recall. Why and how are we alone again? I'm sorry I don't recall. but he's sitting on the couch with me. I remember he impatiently asking me to show him what was under my skirt. After a few… I did. I showed him… I don't remember the face he made or what happened next, but I remember my tiny little white underwear with a purple flower pattern and a purple border in zig-zag stitching.

Another day, and my cousin was there again. I struggled to remember how it all started, how old I was, how wrong it was. We were at Mama Pula's in her outdoor bathroom. I saw his brother, my cousin Jon, sitting outside reading books. I could see him through the wooden wall, and wondered if he could see me in there with his brother. If he knew what we were up to. I'm half naked and he's on his knees, so our bodies are level. I can feel it… feel him.

"*Fulano!*" His friend is screaming for him, looking for him. He calls out to them calmly, and says he'll be right out. He knows what we're doing is wrong, and I notice how he's trained his voice to remain steady and level so as to not give us away. For him, it was just his friend wanting to hang out. For me, I was saved.

"*Vamos a nadar,*" his friend said. *Let's go for a swin*

"*Ta bien manito, ahi voy*" He replies. *Okay, brother. Be right there.*

"*Quadate ahí, no te vallas, porque Jon está afuera y te va a ver.*" He instructs me. *Stay there. Don't go outside because Jon is there.*

He went to meet his friend, acting normal, natural, as if he hadn't just had me in the bathroom. I waited in there, pulling up my little pants and wondering what to do about it all. Jon was still outside reading, and I couldn't wait for him to get up to leave the bathroom. I had a playdate with a friend, and I wanted to go, to be a normal little girl for a while.

I don't know how long I waited, but I remember the look on Jon's face when I finally left the bathroom. I could be wrong, but the way that his heart seemed to skip a beat and his eyes filled with a million years of confusion when he saw me getting out. I had lost track of it all, I just didn't know anymore.

For many, many years, I've not let myself be the victim, be the abused little girl. I've always portrayed myself as a strong, powerful woman. I thought I should have done more, fought him off or ran away or maybe just told my mom. I knew I could trust her, but how could I ruin her in the same was I was ruined? I was always so ashamed, not knowing that I was being taken advantage of, that I didn't do anything wrong. I wasn't just an innocent girl anymore. I'd been forced to grow up. My innocence was taken away from me, and I grew up thinking I had done it to myself. That certainly a six to seven year old decided to find herself in a bathroom with a man that was 15 years older than her.

For so long, I condemned the six-year-old me for being in that position, for taking part in it. He didn't just take my innocence away. He destroyed me. I've hidden behind the idea that I could blame that clueless, tiny version of me for giving something away that I'd never get back. It was part of me now, and would affect the trajectory of the rest of my life.

CHAPTER 6
EVEN IF FAR AWAY FROM HOME, I BELONG

Every summer on the island, after school ended, Pau, Pam, and I went to *campamentos, summer camps;* which were hosted at our school, and we were grouped by age, so I saw a lot of my peers and classmates over the summer. They came up with new activities every day, scavenger hunts and raffles, and different things to keep us entertained. I always enjoyed them, but the year I met Yinauris and Stephanie stood out among the rest. Most years, Julia went to Santo Domingo for a few weeks, and I was left to find other friends. It wasn't hard since we all knew each other, but I still waited anxiously for Julia's return every year.

I started hanging out with some other peers, Yinauris, Genesis, and Stephanie. They were cool, and fun to hang out with. We even had our own handshake. Most days, we'd leave camp together and head to one of our houses or the river to hang out. Stephanie and I were both from Los Patos, and had lived there all our lives. Yinauris was born there, too, but moved to Santo Domingo with her mom and only came back for the summer. Genesis, on the other hand, was from New York, but had come to Los Patos to visit family.

After camp, we would also go to the river to swim. Yinauris always had the cutest bikinis, ones the rest of us couldn't afford. Genesis preferred to swim with her clothes on, embarrassed by the shape of her body. Even then, at the same age as her, I remember thinking she was too young to have such worries. I had a cute bikini my mom's aunt, Celania sent me from the states, but I put shorts over to top of it because I didn't feel comfortable with all the guys around, especially with their unashamed staring. Stephanie was always watching us, sitting on the side of the river but never swimming herself. She was too careful to get her perfect hair wet. This was also her way of reminding me that her mom relaxed her hair before turning 15. After we got tired of swimming and playing in the sand, we'd stop by all of our houses to change, one person running inside while the rest of us hung around on the sidewalk. After, we'd walk to Mama Paula's restaurant. There was always music playing, and we'd sit around and listen as more kids from camp came and went throughout the day. Before it got dark we walked to the beach and grabbed some *fritura.* When we were not at the beach, we were walking around the town looking for mangos or *guava* or any free fruits laying around. Other days, we would go to Stephanie's house to listen and write down our favorite songs, mostly Aventura or Rakim & Ken-Y songs. These were golden afternoons, and they made me forget about my worries. These days I didn't think about growing up and everything that comes with it. I lived in the moment, in the present joy and enjoyed my life and my friends for what they were.

When we were hanging out at Genesis's house, old people would stop by to have her translate the instruction on the back of medicine bottles that the manufacturer wrote in English. I also thought of her as more or superior because she was well traveled and spoke English. But she was humble, sweet, and fun to hang out with. Genesis was my best friend on those summer afternoons.

But summer camp came to an end, and so did our friendships. Genesis went back to New York, and Yinauris went back to Santo Domingo. But, Stephanie and I remained friends. She gave me the secret to convincing my mom to let me relax my hair before I turned 15.

1-Complain about headaches

2-Persistently beg until she gets a headache

3-Wait for her to cave

This camp was one for the book, the memories, the friendships, and the fun we had were always good days. I remember everything about that last year at summer camp. From the smell of the water and the way the sand felt under my feet to the feeling in my stomach after eating a ripe piece of fruit and the way my jaw hurt from laughing so hard. I went to many summer camps, but this is the one I remember vividly. I'll never forget the laughs and the feelings of a great childhood with unforgettable friends.

However, I had a mission after summer camp: Get my hair relaxed. I went out of my way to look depressed and forlorn, as if my world had fallen apart.

To my amazement, Stephanie was right. My mom finally conceded. When I look back at the moment, it feels like just seconds later I was at the salon waiting my turn. Dominicans are top-tier hairstylists, but the amount of gossip that transpires during an appointment is inexplicable. I walked out of there knowing the family's secrets of people I'd never met and not knowing what to do with the information.

When it was finally my turn the stylist called me over. After I sat down, she steps on the treadle and lifted the chair until my hair was level with her hands. I watched her pour the relaxer in a black small container, and stir it. I loved that I was finally going to leave the piggy tails behind me. I wouldn't need my mom to do my hair for me, and I'd have the freedom to style it however I wanted to. The woman slowly started applying the paste to my roots. It was surreal having my childhood dream being fulfilled by a few ounces of chemicals. Further, as she continued to apply it to my hair, I realized that I was crossing over from a girl to a woman during this appointment.

My reverie was quickly interrupted by a kind of blistering pinch on my scalp. I paused for a moment, wondering if it would subside. But then I felt another, this time hotter. It felt as if my stylist had placed a cap full of red hot needles on my head.

She asks me, *"Te pica?"* does it burn?

"No, estoy bien" I replied. *No, I'm fine.*

I felt like I was dying. After what felt like days, the stylist walked me over to the sink and washed out the relaxer. The thought of cool water on my scalp was so relieving. But, in reality, the water only made it worse. The steady stream from the facet felt like lava. A part of me thought when I finally looked in the mirror that all my hair would be gone, burned away by chemicals.

After she washed my hair, she put rollers in it. The sight of her putting something else in my hair made me flinch. But as she started in on the last stage of the process, I felt the heat subside.

When she spun me around to look in the mirror, I saw a different me. I was a woman. A woman with beautiful, long, straight hair. Not a sign of rebel curls, not a sign of *pelo malo* even though my hair was soaking wet. The shrinkage was defeated. I had *pelo bueno* now, I thought, and I instantly felt pretty. I looked more mature and it felt as if the clothes I was wearing too grew up in the last hour with me. I'm grown.

AS I GREW OLDER AND MORE RESPONSI-

BLE, MY MOM would send me to Santo Domingo to her sister's house. Usually, Julia would be there too, as she moved to our aunt's house for an indefinite time.

By then, Julia was at an age where she wanted to experiment and do things I wasn't ready to do. I'm not talking about having the confidence to wear little bikinis and mini skirts and ignore the guys lurking at you. Julia was ready to explore her sexuality and other things that adults do for entertainment. The city life wasn't really that much fun except for the fact that we have access to the internet and better TV channels. We also loved how the lack of exposure to the sun made us look lighter and when we returned to Los Patos, people would say tu *si ta blanca*. Julia would go as far as wearing a hoodie during 100-degree weather to avoid getting tanned when washing and hanging the clothes outside every Saturday.

During our time in Santo Domingo, we would be in the house night and day. It felt like prison sometimes. Our aunt would take us to McDonald's or Burger King. I loved the fake yellow crowns we got from Burger King. Mind you, these don't count as fast-food places in D.R., not everybody can afford to go there. Another fun thing was that we got to do our hair every weekend at the salon.

Julia and I make the best out of our time together. But each summer, when we arrived at our aunt's house, it was almost as if we came with new version of ourselves. Our interests kept changing while we were away.

We went from playing with dolls to not playing with anything at all. We used to spend hours building little houses out of old carton boxes and playing mom and dad. Now, we care more about how our hair, physical appearance and the outfits we wear.

We couldn't go out without putting on lip gloss that made us look like we just ate *chicharron*. Although I was also maturing, Julia was doing so at a faster pace, from her body to her mind. I was somehow okay with it, despite being a little worried about the fact that we were the same age, yet I looked like her little sister.

In 2006, we spent a lot of time on the computer that summer. We took turns using Skype, Instant Messenger, and Hi5. My aunt created an email address for me. so I was able to create my social media accounts when I was 12. While browsing mainly through Hi5, which was a social media before Facebook or Instagram. I saw many people who had moved out of Los Patos. I started to add them and random people so I could seem as cool as some users that had a lot of comments and "nice" photos on their profiles.

Julia had made many friends in La Capital. One was named Janet. She was a lot older than us. She took up educating us on things she thought young girls like us should be doing. In her mind, there seemed to be some arbitrary rule or something, like girls our age should've already dated a guy, or at least gotten some private-intimate actions with someone.

Janet thought it was crucial for us to have a photo shoot so we could update our pictures on Hi5 or in case a guy asked for photos of us on Messenger. So, we agreed. At this stage, I was learning more about beauty standards. These standards were different than my mother's, to whom, I was beautiful. These were more of society's standards. As I understood them more, I started longing for attention based solely on my looks. I noticed men who looked at me on the street and gave me their attention, and I wanted more of it.

At a certain point, Julia started to hang out a lot more with Janet. I became more of an outsider. But even when it was just Julia and me again, it became harder to find ourselves on the same page. Julia was curious about what it felt like to lose one's virginity. I was terrified of the thought. *Why was she so curious? With whom would she do it? How would she do it?* Even though she had gone to school here in La Capital, she didn't know anyone special enough. More than Julia's best cousin/friend, I'm becoming her consciousness. I'm constantly talking her out of doing things, so that she doesn't get in trouble. I'm now the little angel on her shoulder, arguing with the devil on the other side.

Our aunt had a TV in her room, which had an adult package that showed pornography. The only right thing to do was watch it to see if we can gather some ideas or thoughts for her to go off from. As we finished watching, we both stared at the TV, and then at each other, not knowing what we just watched or why it looked so violent. *Also, were the cowboy's boots and hats crucial to the story?* After watching it, I had hoped that it would change Julia's mind.

When we left, I turned off the TV, but forgot one critical detail. I forgot to change the channel. This was early in the day and everything about that day is now blank. We were speechless, the level of distress took days to recover from. But it did not stop her from wanting to lose her virginity.

A few days after, we went to the salon early on a Saturday morning, same as every weekend. Fortunately, we were the first ones, so I went straight back to have my hair washed. When they were doing my rollers, I realized Julia wasn't there, and I wondered where she was. I went under the dryer and, finally, she appeared. Everything seemed normal, and she went to have her hair washed, too. Afterwards, on our way out, she said, "I did it."

"What did you do?" I asked.

"I had sex," she replied.

"WHAT? WHEN? WHO? WHAT?" I yelled, confused and needing answers.

She seemed chill and open to telling me every little detail.

She goes on, "This guy, I went to school with. We dated for a while and I hadn't seen him, but I saw him and it happened."

When we got home, she went to the bathroom to ex-amine her body; to check its response to having sex. She told me that she bled, and that she felt wider. She was now able to fit her thumb inside of herself. To compare, she asked me to try fitting mine inside myself, but it felt like I could barely fit my pinky. She also told me that it hurt, but she had another date with this guy. I didn't even know him, but after this, I honestly couldn't stand him. I knew that if he was special, I would've heard about him.

"WHO WAS IN MY ROOM?" Tia furiously called from the other her bedroom.

We ran to her, clueless, and saw her holding the remote in her hand, her face as red as a tomato. Immedi-ately, we knew what was happening. We forgot to switch the channel. We denied it, and she must have believed us, because she never mentioned it again.

When Tia left for work, Julia started making plans to see her mysterious guy again. I didn't even try to stop her. I knew there was no changing her mind. I wasn't go-ing to stand in the way of anybody's happiness. Besides, *who was she hurting?* I was just relieved to know where she was and what she was doing.

About an hour later, Julia came home crying, saying that she regretted having sex with this guy. She explained that after they had finished, I came up in conversation. He asked if I would be open to having a threesome with them. I was grossed out. So many questions popped into my head. I'd never met this guy. Had he ever even seen me? Or heard of me? I was so creeped out. Julia expressed how used and dirty she felt. To the point where she feels unworthy.

I responded, my voice firm but gentle, "This jerk did not take anything from you or make you less valuable, the complete opposite, you added to him for just giving the privilege of even talking to you." I kept up the same messaging for what felt like hours, trying to make her believe me.

Sadly, school break was coming to an end, and we'd soon be returning to Los Patos. I was low-key excited because I'd get to see my family; my mom and sisters and my dad and dogs. During our last weekend at Tia's house, Julia decided that we should spend on all of the money we'd saved that summer to buy something nice. We went to the store, and she walked straight to the jewelry counter. I didn't think we even had enough to afford to stand here, let alone purchase anything. She picked out a small ring with a Mickey Mouse where there'd normally be a diamond. She then gifted it to me and told me it was a friendship ring for who I am with her. In other circumstances, this would seem a small gesture, but given our lives and how broke we both were, this was the nicest thing anybody had ever done for me.

TIA DROPPED US OFF JULIA AND ME AT THE BUS STOP TO head over to Los Patos. While driving there, I felt relief that I was finally going home, and I didn't have to be in the middle of a traffic war in the city. Driving in the city always scared me because everyone was always rushing and speeding. Each driver was crazier than the next. I was glad I didn't have to deal with that anymore.

The drive to and from the capital is always long. No easy way in or out. The trip is made shorter in a car instead of the public bus; no need to stop for passengers to get on and off every few blocks. And we get to avoid that one person (there's always someone) who gets sick and throws up on the bus. You can always tell who they carry a plastic bag with them, holding it in their laps for the whole trip. They always give themselves away.

Still, bus travel is its own kind of culture. Everyone meets at the main stop. It's like a hub where you come for red *caramelos* sweeter than sugar to *canquiña, dulces* to *cazabe*, and everything in between. All the Dominican candies that all Dominicans love. These are the goodies everyone expects you to bring when coming back from La Capital.

Before the final destination, we make a final glorious stop by one of the biggest organic markets. Technically, we were forced to slow down, by three-back-to-back speed bumps and the dozen vendors entering the vehicle like a Trujillo's ambush to sell their products. You see people buying nuts, and other grapes, but you will always see me buying *manzana de oro* already peeled and salted on a black plastic bag almost custom-made for me. The vendors never had change, so if you had $50 pesos and you wanted to purchase something you had to spend it all. Finally, here it's where you can admire the endless things you can do with different types of wood. beautiful *pilón, tostones smasher*, cups, art, faceless dolls. About three blocks full of unique exhibits and art. I never thought to stop and buy anything from there. I mean, I never thought I'd need to remember or reminisce about a place and things that were always part of me. It was unnatural to even think I'd be away from all of this.

I've made the trip from the capital to home a lot, enough times that I recognize landmarks in the scenery that give me an idea of how far I am from home. Each one brings me closer. The moment I hear the running crystal water and breathe in the pollution-free air, I know I'm home. I see my friend's houses and their neighbors along the main road. I get off at Mama Pula's restaurant, one of the town's busiest bus stops. I put my luggage down, and say hello to each and every person hanging out at the front of the shop. It's a tradition to greet every-one upon your return. If I didn't, they'd label me as *"la anjenta."* After making the rounds, I went back to the old kitchen, where there's always delicious food. Mama Pula always welcomed me back with a smile and a hug, but I sometimes suspected Papa Hombre missed me more.

He'd greet me in his own way, yelling one of the many nicknames he'd given me.

The moment I grab my luggage and start trolling it to my house, I immediately become the sensation of the hour. I thought. I was happy to head home to see mom, but she wasn't even there. She was at her grandma's house, where good coffee was served. Still, I returned to my sisters and cousins and friends and felt like a celebrity among them. With all my new clothes and stories of my adventures, I had so much to share with them I gave them all their gifts, and for the rest of the day we just hung out, sharing stories of our summers. I knew the next morning things would be back to normal. My celebrity appeal would wear off, so for the time being, I relished in it.

In the middle of it all. Summer camps, vacations, the friendships, I was growing up and becoming my own person. I tried my best with the information I had. Becoming a person with dreams. Of course, my dreams only extended as far as my lived experiences would allow. My career goals reached as far as attending the Univesity of Santo Domingo, which my mother and everyone I know attended before me. I spent my days practicing my writing skills on a typographer my aunt let me take with me from La Capital. I was always fond of antiques. To be frank, I smashed my fingers more than I wrote, so after a while I went back to paper. I like to draw, but was at a point where I didn't think odd hobbies were a good use of my time. Still, I had notebooks full of random artwork, proof that it was still a big part of my life.

I stayed busy with my friendship with Julia, trying to catch up with her about our summers. It became too much work. My friendship with Stephanie became solid and less exhausting than my friendship with Julia. I was less stressed and anxious with her and I had more space to be myself. Nonetheless, my bond with Julia was solid too, except when a more daring person came along that would accompany her on all her adventures. I was always there when she needed to tell someone her secrets or indulge her curiosities or get her out of trouble. She was curious to try weed. Some guy who liked her hooked her up. She told me after she had it, huddled in the bathroom together, her smoking while her parents

were talking in the other room. I lost her for a few hours.
I freaked out when her mom knocked in the bathroom,
and I needed to get her out of there without them noticing that she was high. I kept telling her to act normal.
While I put some random eye drops in her eyes, hoping
it would help with the red eyes, and sprayed perfume
all over to get rid of the smell. I then pretended we were
doing our makeup and that's why we were laughing.

Because everyone knows we're like sisters, I was
always as nervous about her parents finding out about
her antics as I was my own. The biggest scandal yet was
when she had run out with her new boyfriend and didn't
come back until late. Her dad was furious and asked
me where she was. I told her to be back by nine, but she
wasn't. I couldn't cover anymore, and I didn't know what
to say, so I started crying and begged her dad to be easy
on her. It was 11:00 PM and we were all sitting around
waiting for her to appear. Just before midnight, we saw
her approaching the house, slowly walking toward us,
knowing she'd been busted. She tried to play it off but
her dad wasn't buying it. He hit her with a force I had
rarely seen before. Sometimes, I wished I was as cool as

her, but I didn't want the same kind of trouble she caused for herself. No fun in the world was worth disappointing my mother.

She's always been the crazy type. But I have been through life with her, and I love her. From childhood to being on a plane to a complete foreign county to now, just before she becomes a mom and close to graduate from high school. Our families lived separately by then, but we were closer than ever.

Most of the time, I feel left out, and in most conversations, I don't know what the heck Americans are talking about with the childhood references and fancy food names. I can always learn more about a culture, but in my childhood, I had to live it. I can go back to my country and everything still feels familiar. I'm no stranger to my roots. I understand it's not part of my future entirely, but it's part of my past that comes to life every time I fly back. It comes back to life every time I bring pieces of D.R. in the form of Dominican cheese, *dulce de leche*, and Dominican chips packed in a suitecase.

CHAPTER 7

THE FRIENDSHIP RING

Now I'm here in a whole different life trying to find myself. Exploring the new parts of me that a new life bring. But also, reconnecting with the parts of me that I lost when I didn't know any better. I never used to care much about the daily mail delivery, but after applying to Kean University in the spring, I started checking the mail every day, waiting for a response. Even though it wasn't my intention to attend, I still longed for their validation. I wanted to know that it was possible that I could be accepted there, and that a decision not to go was my own doing. One day, I see a white envelope sitting on the dining table, with the circled logo perfectly centered on the back of the envelope. Everyone knew I've been waiting for this, so my mom probably separated it from the rest of the mail to the side. I was immediately hopeful that I'd be accepted.

I quickly grabbed the envelope and ripped it open, being careful not to harm the neatly folded paper inside.

I unfolded the letter. Suddenly it hit me; if they accepted me I'd have to go, and if they didn't I'd have to deal with the disappointment of not being enough for them. They used a nice san serif font and left-aligned text that makes it easier to read and follow. Instead of reading it out loud, I let my heart read it. Slowly, I opened the letter and read:

Dear Rafaela,

While we thank you for your interest in Kean University, we cannot offer you a placement… yada yada. However, after reviewing your application, we're pleased to tell you that you've been selected as one of our applicants to be granted a position on our wait list… etc. etc.

I stood silent for a few minutes, letting the information wash over me. It felt silly to be so disappointed in something I expected, something I didn't even want in the first place, but I was. I put the letter in the trash, wondering if my exam results would impact my spot on the waitlist.

I walked into my bedroom and took out my phone to

text G.

Me: I feel blue…

G: What's wrong?

Me: I'm anxious about not passing the state exams to graduate high school.

G: Oh sorry to hear that. It's going to be okay. Try to do something to take your mind off things

G: Did you hear back from KU?

Me: Yes, thank you

I ignored his question, because KU is off the table for me now.

G: You're going to be okay princess

I'll admit, the nickname was cringey enough to throw me off for a minute, but I still found it cute.

G: What are you doing?

Before I could finish a message to him, I fell asleep.

G: Are you mad at me?

G: Did you get your graduation dress yet beautiful?

I suddenly jumped up. My phone was ringing and I saw it was an incoming call from G. I was freaked out. We'd never talked on the phone before and I didn't have time to practice. I answered, feeling awkward and nervous about this new developing in our relationship.

"Why didn't you text me back?" G asked, without so much as a "hello."

"Sorry, I was napping." I responded.

He paused before continuing, "I was wondering if it'd be okay if I bought you your graduation dress, as a gift. We could go to the mall to get it together tomorrow."

The kindness of his gesture improved by day ten times over. I thanked him for the offer and told him that, though I appreciated it, I wasn't sure if I wanted him to do that for me. I still wasn't even sure whether I'd passed the state exams to be able to graduate, and wanted to see what my status was before I started celebrating graduation.

"Okay, cool bye," he said, and ended the conversation.

WHEN I GOT TO SCHOOL, I SAW ALL THE seniors lining at the main hallway, waiting to check the notice with our exam results. Some walked away calmly, others jumping with excitement. I was worried I wouldn't be able to hide my reaction if it was bad news for me, so I instead walked right by the results board and into my first class.

A little while later, I got a text from Star.

Star: Hey did you check your score? I didn't see you this morning.

Me: No, I didn't want to see them yet.

Star: Come meet me and the twins in the hallway.

As I approached them, I could see their barely contained smiles. I was suddenly very aware of my own breathing, noticing what each inhale and exhale felt like in my body. I took one last deep breath and searched the board for my name.

I passed. *I did it, Mom.*

I decided to text G.

Me: Do you want to go to the mall?

G: You passed, beautiful!!! Yes, let's go

I told my sisters and Star that G had offered to buy my graduation dress and that we were planning to go to the mall after school. They asked if they could come with us, wanting to help pick out the perfect dress. I thought G would be cool with it, but when I asked he backed down from our plan completely, acting as if something had come up. I tried to convince him. He offered to buy my dress and I didn't have much money. But he wouldn't give in.

G: I really just wanted to go with you only. I think I'll pass

Me: Okay, that's fine. Thank you.

It didn't feel like my place to be angry with G. I was mostly upset because I didn't have the money for a dress, and was too embarrassed to admit it to my sisters or Star. I looked down at my friendship ring from Julia and decided that I could find a jewelry store to sell it. They gave me $50 for it, but the money didn't make me feel better. If anything, I was feeling worse. I had this ring for so long and it was the hardest thing to give it up because I was covering for G's actions.

JULIA AND I WERE SET TO GRADUATE TOGETHER, and I was so proud. In fact, I was beyond proud of her. We had done the whole thing together. We made appointments to get our hair and makeup done for graduation. We ordered our gowns. We were ready.

The moment I sat on the chair and the stylist looked at my hair, I knew I was going to hate the style I chose. She washed my hair and then started with the rollers.

She was using the smallest rollers, and I worried how they'd cause my hair to lose too much length. I started to panic, thinking that if I truly hated it as much as I feared I was going to, I'd have to miss graduation. I'm the type at a salon that would walk out graciously with a shaved head, not expressing any discomfort until the salon door swings shut. I thought this would be more the same, but as she got further along I realized I loved the style and knew it would go well with my dress.

Julia's hair suited her just as perfectly, and we got up from our chairs to head home and get ready. She was glowing, pregnant with her ex-boyfriend's baby, and looking as alive as ever. I couldn't believe that I'd made it. I kept noticing myself in the mirror as we got ready, my cheap shoes and dress that somehow looked elegant on my newly educated body. Our families kept running in and out of the room while we were getting ready, showing their support with their own specific kind of chaos.

The ceremony was long and hot. It felt like the hottest summer, especially with the sun beating down on us. When they called us on stage, a few people danced

around after being handed their diplomas. They weren't
sure if they'd make it, and I understood the sentiment. I
myself was very happy to receive my diploma. It felt like
evidence that God is real.

The idea of not being able to get a higher education
frustrated me to the point where I started losing weight;
I was only 90 pounds, I couldn't afford to lose weight.
But I did; I was down to 87 pounds. Because of school,
yes, but also because I was heartbroken. I hadn't talked
to G since the dress incident, so I decided to stalk him on
social media. He was not difficult to find since we went
to the same high school. When I finally got to his page,
I could not believe my eyes. He had not just one, but multiple girlfriends and it didn't matter how far in the past
I went into his timeline. His page was overloaded with
flirtatious interactions with random girls. I remember
loging on and crying for a month straight. I knew I had to
confront him about it.

G: *sends link to a song*

G: They don't mean anything, you're different

Me: Please get away from me.

I was hoping that would be the end of it.

PEOPLE HAD BEEN ASKING WHAT COL-LEGE I WAS GOING to, and I decided to tell them that I was planning on taking some time off. I thought if I said it enough, I would make my own peace with it. My last choice and perhaps the easiest, was to enroll at the community college, but I wasn't too excited about it. I just felt like it would be like going to another high school. When I told my friend Star about my one-year gap plan, she was the only one able to see through my words and notice how scared I was. She gave me the advice to start at the local community college for now while I got ready for a bigger school.

"It would be better to obtain some credits at the community college, and then next year, you can transfer." She advised and then added, "You'll have a lot of reasons not to do this, but none of them is good enough to stop you from starting now." The day before classes were due to start, the community college held a workshop at our high school gym. They were helping people apply correctly and accepting applications on the spot. I decided to go, and when I got there, there was a long line that stretched across the room. When I finally approached the table and told the lady working it that I wanted to register and start classes tomorrow, she gasped. Apparently, I wasn't the only one who thought this was a rushed decision. But it worked. The process that had taken months before was now over in just a few hours. I registered for classes, applied and was approved for financial aid, and that was it. I was officially a college freshman.

They advised me to start taking ESL classes and then transfer into my major, which worked out because I wanted to become a history teacher and technically, that wasn't an option in the school. I started taking writing classes and reading classes. I met wonderful people, many of whom were just like me and my family. They'd come to this country as kids, parents, grandparents, aunts, uncles, and cousins. They were taking steps to further their education, and we worked together on it. College was the place where my English improved the most. Star and I started hanging out during my time at the community college, and she introduced me to *Friends*. I will always love her for this, not only because it helped improve my English, but because I genuinely enjoyed the show.

The local community college, was located just a few blocks from our apartment building, so I was able to walk every day or take the dollar bus. I enjoyed the walk, always with my headphones on, which gave me time to daydream. I got to distract myself from checking G's profile every second, and slowly I started getting over him. It was hard to have to give up everything he offered me and the idea of being with someone.

One day, when I was walking home from class, a man in a car approached me and asked for directions. Even though I had no idea what to tell him, I thought of this as an opportunity to practice my English. I leaned forward to tell him I was sorry and that I didn't know how to direct him. That's when I noticed that he didn't need directions, his pants were off, and he was holding the wheel with one hand and his penis with the other, watching me the whole time. Suddenly, the traffic light changed and he drove away.

I stood frozen for a few seconds, unable to react and trying to make sense of what had just happened. None of it made sense so, I continued to walk home. As I entered my house, my mom noticed something was wrong and started asking questions. I didn't tell her, partly because I was embarrassed to but also because our home was full of friends and relatives that day. My mom took me into the bathroom and I finally broke down. I told her what had just happened and she was furious, speechless, and helpless. We both were.

I never saw that man again, but I can still remember his face like he was someone I'd always known. I remember what he looked like, the false kindness with which he approached me, even the jeans he was wearing. Most of all, I remember my disgust and my anger, how violating it was for this man to assume that I would just accept his actions.

The day after the incident, I walked again to school, but was trying to be more careful about who I talked to. Everyone always told me I was from the hood. That I needed to watch out for gangs and drugs. Walking to school went on for a long time, and I had the opportunity to learn more and more English.

THE DIFFICULTY OF STUDYING HALF GRADES IN AMERICA AND half grades in the Dominican Republic was that I never completed some lessons necessary for a well-rounded vocabulary in either language. I always felt behind in academia. I was conditioned to try hard to get rid of the accent and learn English and I abandoned Spanish. God forbid I tried to speak in Dominican Spanish; nobody would understand me. But I was accused of trying too hard when I intended to speak Spanish without Dominican slang. Too often I had to translate what I'd learned in the D.R. to English or vice versa. Interestingly enough, both my English and Spanish feels incomplete, and it often shows. It made me insecure, so much so that I felt like people could hear my lack of confidence in my words. I grew anxious and hopeless. I held myself back a lot, silence the preferred alternative to sounding stupid. Being part of two worlds brings challenges that must be overcome, but I wouldn't have it any other way. I continued to learn more about the American culture while at the same time appreciating my native culture more than I ever did before.

My time at the community college was essential to my journey of learning the language and connecting with people of similar backgrounds. But my favorite part was how my relationship with Star grew. She was taking a class at my school while she finished her last year of high school, and I'd often get to see her at the library. Most days we went there to study, but sometimes we'd just sit back and talk about *Friends*, about Ross and Rachel's break up, about how they were not on a break.

CHAPTER 8

COLLEGE LIFE

In high school, I always tried to stay hidden. I avoided sports and after-school programs, anything that would require me to socialize or put me in front of my peers. The community college made it even easier to hide in plain sight.

A year into my studies, my sisters started applying to schools themselves. Both were interested in business degrees, so Mr. PJ suggested they apply to Berkeley College. It's one of the best business schools in the country, and I was thrilled that they were accepted.

When I started my search for a new school, my sisters suggested I check it out. We thought it would be fun to all go to the same school. I agreed and set up a meeting with an admissions counselor to see if I would be eligible.

I always knew I wanted to do something that'd help humanity and would be invaluable to those around me, like teaching or perhaps being some sort of counselor. Of course, I always loved art, but I saw it as a form of self-expression designed to benefit myself more than others. I didn't think it was an acceptable career choice, until the counselor I met with introduced me to graphic design. It was the closest thing to being an artist. I didn't know exactly what direction it would take me in, but I knew everything revolved around design, and I was excited. It was part art and part problem solving. I enrolled.

I applied for financial aid and, due to my mom's status as a "single mom" while my dad remained in the Dominican Republic. I was accepted. I was also offered several other scholarships that would help me complete all four years without having to owe anything afterward. It seemed like all the obstacles standing between me and an education vanished. I now just had to overcome my social anxiety and master my still-broken English. During my admissions meeting, it was suggested that I take a free summer course for new students, meant to help me meet new people and get used to college course work. Realizing how beneficial it would be, I took the opportunity.

Orientation day was a success. I got to meet the Director of the graphic design program and a bunch of other students that were also interested in enrolling. I sat in the front row, one of the first to arrive to orientation. I was so afraid to be noticed that I held myself back from coughing, so much so that when I took a sip of my water, I choked. I choked on water. I hated that I was so afraid of being seen, of being me, as if the mere idea of me was a sin. I wanted to give myself the freedom to enjoy the opportunity that was given to me without feeling the need to apologize for who I was; who I am. It was the broken English that made it the hardest. Just because my words were a little jumbled didn't mean they weren't worth hearing.

While the Dean was showing us all what the program was going to be about, I couldn't help but notice her appreciation for all types of art. She spoke of pieces that depicted history, and how the brilliant colors and shapes revealed details about each artist's life. She even spoke of the more controversial art; the kind that highlights injustice and brings awareness to other people's suffering. Despite having no idea what I was getting into, I realized that Berkeley could help me achieve my dreams. I didn't even know exactly what my dreams were at the time, but

I knew I was on my way.

MY FIRST DAY FELT JUST LIKE THE OLD DAYS. On the first day of classes, it dawned on me that new starts weren't exactly my area of expertise. We start by watching the Helvética Documentary because it would've been blasphemy if we didn't. Helvetica is one of the must used and loved fonts among great designers. When we started talking about Comic Sans I looked around the room. Everyone hated it. Without even really knowing why, I decided I'd hate it, too. It was a diverse group of students in that classroom, and knowing that helped me feel less anxious. I still wanted to be invisible, but it felt possible I'd come out of my shell, even just a small bit.

The professor's named was Avery. She was nice and innovative, both of which I remembered from orientation. After a bit, we signed into Adobe Illustrator and she walked us through every tool. Our first assignment was to draw a digital portrait. We had a week to work on it, and when I looked around at the other student's progress, I was embarrassed by my work. I didn't know if it was just because I was awful or because I didn't have a computer at home, but I soon fell behind. When asked to present our portrait, I was mortified to see my work hung beside everyone else's. I wondered how I would survive in a major that required me to showcase my work to the other students. It seemed to do little more for me than add to my current anxieties.

Professor Avery really went all out for us. She planned a trip to the MET for the following month. I was excited. It would be my first time ever visiting the MET and New York City. News of the trip helped get me through the next few weeks. It seemed all my new assignments went as poorly as the first. Still, I was making friends who helped me along the way.

Despite each class following the same routine, they never felt repetitive. I struggled with the thought of what I might end up doing with this degree in the real world, but I tried to enjoy myself and the experiences I was living.

I loved my design classes because they never felt like real work. Unlike my other classes, where I really had to bust my butt and work hard. Especially my bio-ethics class with Professor Abuchaba. Perfect vocabulary, smart brain, good-looking, all-around deserving of the crush I had on him. His soothing voice and smart words were like a sweet melody to my life. I needed it. After the scary class syllabus he handed out, I was surprised to love his class, though it was probably for the many deep conversations that took place in his class. Even some of the conversations that were more sensitive and exciting to engage in.

One period, after watching a documentary on legalizing euthanasia, Professor Abuchaba open up a discussion about what we'd just watched. Before he could even finish his introduction, a girl at the back of the class shouted, "This is a sin and you're going to hell if you do it!" The rest of the class had to stifle their laughter, but Professor Abuchaba responded to her gently, and then moved the discussion along. At the end of that class, he reminded us that we were to give a final presentation in a few weeks. My fears suddenly rushed back to me.

MET DAY IS HERE! I COULDN'T WAIT. IT FELT like the most fantastic day of my life. The first train ride to the city was smooth, but the second seemed to be full of reckless people. It reminded me of the public buses in the D.R., always full beyond capacity. As long as the door was closed, they'd call it operational. After the train we then had to walk many blocks to get to the MET. I didn't mind the walk because I certainly needed time to admire the city and the beautiful architecture that surrendered me.

We finally walked up to the most stunning, aesthetical-perfect building. Its high columns just screamed history. We went through the entry, showed our tickets, and walked into the first gallery. Already, I was in love with the place and its rich history. I followed closely behind a private tour, learning as much as I could about the art and the artists.

The MET filled me with hope. My appreciation for art grew deeper than I could have dreamed. I realized that there isn't good or bad art. There is art that carries years of history and art that affects social change; art that makes a person feel strongly connected to the artist. How well a piece of artwork tells a story is what really defines whether it's good or bad. Beyond all, art is a form of personal storytelling, and I knew it was what I wanted to do for the rest of my life.

When it came time to walk out, I got the feeling that I needed more time to be with all the beautiful exhibitions. Rene, another new student, was also hanging back with me, trying to delay her departure. Eventually I realized it was alright to leave, mostly because I knew I would be back some day. When we stepped outside, I could feel the energy of the thousands of New Yorkers walking the same street as me. It was like a palpable buzz of energy. It was the perfect place to be anonymous because no one cared about your life, only their own. I started to day-dream about living in New York and what it would be like. I knew I wasn't ready, but I saw it in my future. For now, I'd stay back home and attend college, which I knew was right where I needed to be.

EACH DAY MY SISTERS AND I HAD TO WALK to take the shuttle, which gave me the extra time I needed to reflect and listen to some music. We walked through what most would consider "the hood." I looked at the people, my neighbors. Often, going somewhere, hurrying to get somewhere. I was told many things about "the hood", but one thing I know is this is where I met the most determined and hard-working people I know.

The free shuttle ride to school was a blessing, but also a tortorous silence. Everyone had their eyes locked on their phones, the silence somehow made more deafening by the quiet communication between person and phone. When the bus arrived everyone scattered to walk to their classes. I always walked to my design classes with excitement, knowing I would either get to create something new or be introduced to a new kind of art or artist. We learned that our next trip would be to NYC's Comic Con. I didn't even know what it was, but I was excited to go back to my favorite place.

My classmates were discussing whether or not they were going to dress up. I listened in, nervously, knowing I didn't have any formal clothes. While they sat talking, I nervously Googled "Comic Con" to see what I could find out. I laughed when I realized it wasn't a formal party, and shuddered imagining showing up in a gown while everyone else wore a pair of animal ears. Thank God for Google.

When we arrived at Comic Con, we had to wait in a long line outside to get in. We stood around admiring the funny costumes, wondering what the day would hold.

Upon entering, I realized it was just as rich of an atmo-
sphere at the MET, just in a totally different way.

I HAD MY FIRST REAL DESIGN INTERVIEW
AFTER JUST a few months. Of all the projects I'd designed so far for Professor Av's class, I still didn't think
any were much better than a children's drawing. The
company Movado had come to the school looking for a
Jr. Graphic Designer. They encourage everyone to get in-
terviewed at school. Though, I did not feel ready, I decided to go for it. The interview took place at school and by
two female Movado staff. This made it a lot easier for me.

At the interview, I sat down and handed my portfolio to the two women I'd be speaking with. I let them
conduct the interview while I sat back and felt extremely
intimidated by them. It was rather embarrassing to show
the poor work I've done in the short period of time. I
think they noticed my lack of confidence, by the way
they complimented my work. I feel small and pitied. I
kept my answers short to save us all some time. It was
no surprise to see the rejection letter a few weeks in the
mail. It scared me, making me think I was headed toward
a life of rejection. I had been told before that I'd selected a

competitive major, but I had to keep going. It was what I felt I truly loved.

Once, during 3D design class, Professor Av came in with another professor and introduced him to us all individually. When she came to where I was sitting, my heart started racing so fast and loud that I failed to hear what she'd said. I made some noncommital agreement, but could tell by the look on her face she was expecting more from me. As it happens, she was saying goodbye. Professor Av would be leaving, and this new person was her replacement. I had been comfortable with Professor Av, and was suddenly saddened that she didn't care as much as she originally said she did. This is a great opportunity for her, but for me it was another anxiety-inducing fresh start. I looked for her after class to say a proper goodbye, and when she left she said she couldn't wait to see the great things I'd do. I wasn't entirely sure what she meant, my English was still pretty broken and my work wasn't any better. But I had a feeling that she could see my potential beyond my poor presentations and design work.

Roger, the new professor to replace Professor Avery, started off his first class with a game of Wink Murder. He wrote two names on small pieces of paper; one would be the murderer, and the other the detective. He joked that some people might not be good at the game, especially if English wasn't their first language. I don't know if he expected the class to laugh, but nobody did. Everyone was sitting in a circle, eyeing one another up, trying to determine who the murderer might be. It was me. I tried to act natural, tried to blend in the way a real killer would. Everyone stared at each other nervously, laughing and trying to come to the right conclusions. No one suspected me. Eventually, there were just three of us left, and the detective guessed the wrong person. I won the game. I supposed non-English speaking students weren't so bad at the game after all.

Despite being a little awkward, it was a great exercise to break the ice. He proceeded to show us his portfolio, including his work for Sesame Street. A beautiful brand guideline that seemed like fun to create. The more he showed us, the more my future in the world of design felt possible. But his class was more demanding than Professor Av's, and I had to spend extra hours at school finishing up projects.

One afternoon, I decided to stay up late to do some homework. I walked into a night class held by a very friendly white guy. He approached me and asked me what I was working on. He took an interest in my work and decided to help, offering me some tips. I decided to enroll in his class, and Rene came, too. After the rest of the class was gone, we met Patrick, another new and friendly professor, who shared some of his experiences with us, offering advice on designs and how to make good money from them. I was thankful to have met Patrick. He was kind and inspirational, always leaving me feeling inspired to thrive. Though his voice was very dominating, it was also gentle and humble. The passion for design that he spoke with was palpable.

In our next class with Roger, we were assigned a project to take an existing brand and make it into something completely bad or wrong. I decided to rebrand *Forever21* as if it was a store that sold adult diapers. We laughed through the creatively deceptive brands curated by my classmates. Rene had a tuna fish candle which was absolutely histerical. Someone else came up with a gum that replaced brushing your teeth. Everybody else was extremely funny, and when it was my turn I pretended not to have completed the assignment. Once again, I didn't think my work was good enough.

During class one day, we got to know Professor Roger a bit more — more than I'd like. He was reaching up to erase the board, and his shirt raised up, revealing a butterfly tatto on the small of his back. We all stared at each other in silence, wondering if what we'd just seen was real. I could tell people were trying not to laugh just by the look in their eyes. It was very unexpected. He faced us again, completely unaware that we all knew about his tattoo. He handed out an article for us to read aloud as a group. I was terrified, but soon realized that a lot of my classmates struggled to read, even those who grew up speaking only English. I was chosen to read a small paragraph, and you could hear the fear in my voice.

WHEN I SAW PROFESSOR PATRICK ENTER THE CLASSROOM FOR the next lesson, I was relieved. With him we didn't just learn; we had a really good time. He started with a real-world example of the process of designing a logo. The first step is to create up to 50 or more concepts in black and white, and then start removing the bad ideas. You then rework the existing concepts until you had something worthy of the brand it'd be attached to. And so, our first assignment was to come up with a new company and create the basic assets needed to grow. From the brand identity, to letterhead, brochures, a website, etc. In the first week, we were instructed to come up with our 50 logo concepts. I was excited to get started.

In the next class with Professor Patrick, every student printed out their logos and mounted them on the walls. Patrick looked at all of our logos and was entirely unimpressed. He said the logo shouldn't be complicated or complex, instead that logos should be simple and straightforward. They are the solution to the problem. As he critiqued my concepts, he chose one that he said could develop into a great idea.

Patrick's class was the one that hit me. It was tough, taking me forcibly out of my shell. It kept me active, and never let me get lazy. I could no longer hide to cover my weaknesses.

The company I designed for his class was IYO, a yoyo company that donated to the less fortunate. After a whole semester of designs and feedback and reworks, it was the first thing I felt truly proud of. I always kept it at the front of my portfolio because, despite not being a real company, it was something I was proud of.

By this point, I had started to come out of my shell. I felt confident in popular culture, steadily cruising through *Friends* and some of the books my friends talked about. My outfits were better. I was still shy around new people, but was learning to open up. I felt like I was catching up to my design peers, too. College was hard enough as is, but struggling to make people understand me only made it harder. Still, I could tell my experiences were adding up to something great.

CHAPTER 9

FRIENDSHIPS FOR A LIFETIME

The first long-distance train trip I took by myself
was to see my friend Star at The College of New Jersey,
in Trenton. I miss her ever since she moved away. As
I looked out the windows at the scenes we were passing on the train, I felt like we were moving at lightning
speed. Houses and people and trees flashing by. I was
nervous about being alone, sitting next to a bag of Dominican groceries Star's dad had sent for her. As the train
stopped, I got ready to disembark so I could catch my
next train. The train station was so massive and I had no
idea where to go. I was trying to ask people for help, my
mom on the phone the whole time, reminding me what a
bad idea this was. But there I was, all on my own.

Finally, I made it to my destination and found Star
waiting for me. She apologized for the bag of groceries as
soon as she grabbed it, but I was just relieved I had made
it to the right place.

We were waiting for another bus to head to her dorm

at her school. While we waited, we sat down to catch up a bit. It was the end of the semester, and we were both just happy to breathe. I looked at her as the bus was pulling in, noticing for the first time how beaten up she looked. She had just gotten out of her final class, and I was hopeful that our weekend of fun would help us both loosen up a bit.

We talked the whole bus ride about *Friends* and how much we enjoyed every episode. It helped pass the time quickly, and before I knew it we'd arrived. We walked to Star's dorm which she shares with another girl. She had a poster of the show Breaking Bad on her wall, another one of my favorite shows she's recommended.

Star showed me around her school, and I noticed very few Black or Hispanic people, which made me feel out of place. When we got to the food court, the line was over-whelming. We ran into a curly-haired girl who seemed to be friends with Star. I was not surprised. My favorite thing about our friendship is that Star constantly intro-duces me to new people and new things, without ever judging my shyness or lack of experiences. This time around, she wanted me to try Chipotle, which, according to her, is the best thing since sliced bread. I was a bit hesitant, realizing that I didn't have much money to spend. She was in no better place than me. We were college students, after all. We came up with a plan that would allow us to do fun things for my whole stay without overspending. We entertained the idea of walking to Chipotle, but it was 30 minutes away. We both agreed that, rather than spend the money for transportation, it was doable. We would have to walk on the highway, but it wasn't the worst thing trip I'd ever trekked. We made a playlist for our way there, but the music didn't stop us from screaming every time a car passed by.

We arrived at Chipotle and my social anxiety returned. I didn't realize I'd have to tell the worker every individual ingredient I wanted, so I decided to just follow Star's lead.

"White rice, chicken, red beans…"

The white girl hesitated, "I'm sorry?"

"Red beans," I replied.

She then smiled and said, "Pinto beans."

Didn't know we had to be so technical, I thought. I of course knew the proper name for pinto beans, but in the

D.R. we only ever call them red beans. Anyway.

I was used to a different kind of food, so what was in front of me honestly looked a little gross. I was used to eating all those foods, but usually each item was separate, not all mixed together like that. We decided to walk back to eat at Star's dorm. I was thinking maybe eating the food wasn't worth the risk. I thought I would hate it, but Star told me I had to try it.

When we got back, we heated the food up a bit. I felt like I had to neglect years of norms and culture, my ancestors and every Dominican I knew.

I tried it.

I loved it.

I was hooked. I couldn't believe an American chain could make red beans that tasted just like my grandmas', but they did. Right then, it became one of my favorite places to eat.

The night was young, and we were planning to stay in for a night of board games. But first, Star snuck in a bit of wine. I had a sip, and it felt like enough to keep me lit for the whole weekend. The laughter it caused made for a good time.

We went to the common area which, again, was filled with a lot more white people than I was used to seeing. I don't think I had seen that many white people since National History Day in high school. I felt like no one saw me for anything other than my appearance. I could feel the tension like a physical thing, growing each time I noticed someone staring at me.

We played pool for a while, and then visited the gift shop. I got her a sweater, which made me go over budget already. Star took me to every corner of her school. The art building on campus got my attention. They had students' work up on the walls, proudly displayed for everyone to admire. I wondered if they had a presentation and critique component like at my school, where all the other artists can tear your work apart; in a good way. I started pointing out the most well-designed pieces and other works that stood out the most to me.

I felt proud of Star and how well she had handled the transition to college life. I left Trenton thinking that I couldn't wait for the great things she would accomplish there. Every semester, it became our tradition to spend a weekend together, escaping the real world and coming back to our lives together. It was always something to look forward to. I admired her decision to stay in the dorm and try to do this thing called adulting.

CHAPTER 10

TO BE YOUNG IN NEW YORK

NYC was an experience. One of the best gifts this country has given me has been allowing me to earn an education without owing thousands of dollars that would take more than a lifetime to pay off. It was still a long process to apply every semester, but it was always worth the time.

I'm now only a few semesters from finishing up the program. The school presented us with internship opportunities, some of which were paid, and many of which could eventually turn into a job. Some of my classmates had landed these opportunities, and I was excited to be granted one myself. By then, my confidence was much greater than it had been before, so much so that I was encouraged to go ahead and apply to the offers at hand. Even if I didn't get anything, it was refreshing to believe it was possible. I never understood my own logic, thinking I didn't deserve things others did. I felt like I knew just as much as anyone and certainly worked just as hard, so I applied for one of the internships.

I received a call back and was asked to come in for an interview. I began to prepare and to really give it my best effort. I was determined not to use my broken English as a barrier, as something that made me less worthy of the opportunities afforded to others. For the first in my life, I was embracing the multicultural side of myself. I realized that my broken English was just part of me, and anyone who thought me to be less than because of it was losing out on someone great. Though I sometimes wished I had just been born in the states and could wholly denounce my accent, I realized it would mean giving up so much of who I am. It would mean forsaking my childhood, my skin tone, the island in me, the place where my skin color wasn't a crime, and that is simply too high a price.

I knew some of my classmates were also applying for the same internship as me, but I still had hope. When I drove into New York City for the interview, I was mesmerized by the miles-high buildings. I was even more surprised when I realized one of them was exactly where I was headed.

I walked up to the building where I was interviewing and was immediately taken aback by the beautiful abstract art lining the walls. A tall, middle-aged man dressed in traditional Jewish garb approached, saying my name, "Rafaela," by way of greeting. He said it the same way all Americans do, lacking the long, rolling "r" as we speak it in Spanish. We shook hands and made our way to the conference room to start the interview.

We were joined by two more men, one Black and one Asian. Though I could appreciate the diversity, I couldn't help but be intimidated by the fact that I was interviewing with three men. I found myself craving the gentleness of a woman's words.

I answered all their questions carefully, choosing fancy words that would make me sound smart and informed. I could tell by their responses and expressions that they were impressed, and I was thankful for that. I was relieved to realize that things were going well.

In the elevator after the interview, my hands were shaking so badly that I could hardly contain them. "Miss, are you okay?" asked a friendly guy, smiling concernedly. A handsome friendly guy. In the course of a few seconds, my jitters go away, and I developed a mini crush on him almost effortlessly. I blame it on his flirtatious smile. "Yes, thank you. I just had an interview, and I'm just glad it's over." I replied.

"No kidding? Best of luck!" He responded, waving me off the elevator in front of him. When I stepped back outside, I realized I might actually be more excited than nervous.

I ALWAYS CHECK MY EMAILS FIRST THING IN THE morning. I tried to break the habit by reading an article instead, but while I was waiting for a response from the internship, I couldn't help but open my emails hoping to hear something. One morning, I received an email from my school's finance office alerting me of an issue with my financial aid. They said that I wouldn't be able to register for classes if it wasn't resolved right away, so I got out of bed and headed to campus. I stopped by before class and, thankfully, got everything resolved. Still, it was a reminder that I still hadn't escaped a life of worry, especially when it came to money.

It seemed like things at school were always changing, but I learned to cope with it. The graphic design department had a new set of directors, who seemed to make massive changes the first hour they were hired. They cut back on all the field trips to museums because, apparently, they were taking up too much of the budget. At that point, I was ready to finish school and get out of there. Patrick was also having a hard time adjusting to the new directors. His classes had been cut back, too, so he decided to leave the school. I knew I could survive two semesters without his mentorship, but I was thankful to know we could still email and chat regularly. He was helpful, and I didn't want to lose him entirely.

In the midst of the new staffing transition, I received an email about the internship. I was trying not to get my hopes up, but I was elated at the idea. I was scared to read the email, and before I clicked, tried to remind myself what rejection felt like, just in case. But I did it. I was offered the job. Despite feeling, I must have been the least qualified, I was offered the position! Grace opens doors for those who need them, and I was feeling that power now more than ever.

NYC IS, ARGUABLY, HOME TO THE MOST ASTONISHING ART and design in the country. Every design for every store was beautifully done, so much so that I started to think of the artists as Marvel superheroes of the design industry. I felt excited to have some time to explore the city on my own, indulging in every nook and cranny that interested me. I loved the commute and often utilized it to read a good book or listen to music. The first time I went out for lunch, I saw a man holding a sign that said, "I'm not gonna to lie, I need money for weed." I appreciated the honesty, but still didn't donate. Every part of the city was so amusing. My phone was filled with NYC skyline pictures and cool posters or flyers I saw. But working in the city helped me realize that my home is in Jersey. No matter how much I loved NYC, it would never truly be home.

One night, while staying late at work, I went to the kitchen to grab a snack from the fridge I had saved for later. But it wasn't there. Someone else had, apparently, taken it for themselves. I was frustrated, and just as I was starting to bubble over, the man I had met in the elevator a few weeks prior came in. I was embarrassed, realizing this was the second time he was seeing me lose control. Maybe that's why he remembered me. "I see you got the job," He stated. I paused, look at him, and told him someone had eaten my snack. "What!" He exclaimed as if I said someone had hurt me. He then said, "We have to take somebody else's snack, then. That's just how it works."

I laughed, but told him I couldn't do it. Ignoring me, he grabbed someone else's yogurt from the fridge. I covered my mouth, and my eyes got wide. I couldn't stop laughing.

"You're a criminal! Let's go," I yelled, while running back to my office. He followed me, still holding the yogurt, and when we got to my office he handed it to me. Because he was so brave and so kind, I couldn't tell him that I don't like yogurt. I thanked him and even ate a few bites to show my appreciation.

"You're welcome," he said, and started to walk away.

"What's your name?" I asked. He turned around and, before I knew it, Alain and I were having a whole conversation. He also lived in Jersey and was only coming to the office temporarily. We shared a nice night together, which I was thankful for. After that, I never saw him at the office again.

But it was okay. My life was complicated enough
with school. My family life was unraveling, too. My mom
accidentally let me in on a secret; I had a little brother.
A half brother, really. A child of my father's back in the
D.R. who had a different mother than my sisters and I.
It was a common enough occurrence on the island, but I
still never thought my father was capable of doing such
a thing to our family. Dominican fathers really just get
tired of sitting around watching the news, and decide to
start a new family.

My sisters took it well. Or, at least, they pretended
they were alright to stay strong for the rest of us. My
mother, however, was devastated and humiliated. As was
I. I had always been a daddy's girl, and now I felt like
I didn't want to look him in the eye. I hid in a Dunkin'
Donuts day in and day out, focusing on my schoolwork
and internship while avoiding my family. In the midst of
all the chaos, I received an email from my boss:

Hello Rafaela,

Hope this email finds you well. (For the record, it didn't.)

I'm sorry to inform you that our office is being relocated *to Bricks, NJ. You're welcome to come along, and, if you agree, we'd like to offer you a design position at our new location.*

I was saddened by the news, but I couldn't even consider the idea of moving away. It was too far from me to be able to commute, and I knew I wanted to finish my degree.

A few days later, I went back to the office to clear out my stuff. When I got there, I found a note with my name on it slipped under my office door. Luckily, the other three people I shared the space with were already gone. It was from Alain; he included his phone number and asked me to call him.

I did. I called, and he asked me to meet up to chat. I told him it was not a good time. I was at Dunkin' doing homework, though it was really just an excuse to get away from my family. I had just met the guy, and I didn't want to dump all my problems on him. But, I told him which Dunkin' I hunged out at every day and that he could feel free to stop by.

He did the next day. Unfortunately, he had gotten a

flat tire and needed some help. I had the tools, not that
I've ever used them myself, but now I finally had the
chance. I hoped that lending him my tool would show
him that I was strong and independent. I wanted him to
see me as smart and capable.

When his car was fixed he thanked me, and then suggested we go out for a proper date. I caved. I suggested
we go to IHOP, and on our way there, he made an illegal
U-turn, and we got pulled over. He handled the situation
calmly and wasn't angry that our date got ruined as I
felt. Later, we realized that the IHOP had burned down. I
took it as a sign that maybe, we weren't meant to be.

A week after, Alain texted me again, saying I still
owed him a date and he knew just the place. I agreed,
and we went to IHOP to finally have our first official
date. We spent the whole night talking about each other's
lives. We were so enamored with each other that we lost
track of time. I was comfortable telling about all my troubles, and was thankful to have such a kind outlet for such
things. He told me about his two favorite books, "Conversations with God" and "The 48 Laws of Power."

After the night ended, I told him how great I thought

he was and that I hadn't had such a peaceful moment in a long time. But I also told him that I wasn't looking for anything beyond friendship and to please respect my space. He smiled and confidently replied, "I'm going to marry you." I laughed at how presumptuous he was for saying that after what I had just told him.

CHAPTER 11

I HAVE A NINE-TO-FIVE

Regardless of the love I had for school, I still found it overwhelming. I could barely meet the deadlines, and yet I was constantly being given new ones. Assignments on assignments, it all piled up with no regard for my personal or social lives. My life felt like a broken record, the same thing over and over again, only wearing down more with each passing day. Except I couldn't stop; I had to keep going. My anxiety made it hard to breathe, and I was regularly bursting into tears from the stress of my day-to-day life. No matter how hard I tried to keep it together, some days, I just couldn't stop the meltdowns. School was, undoubtedly, a blessing. But that doesn't mean it wasn't difficult.

When I thought of the future, I could still see my-self walking through the crowded and tight streets of NYC, so I didn't bother applying to any jobs in Jersey. There was something about New York that always made me feel welcome. Not having a job any longer gave me time to focus on school. Morning, noon, and night I was working. It was my most challenging semester—mostly because of the advanced writing class I was in. It was, admittedly, my favorite. But I was still struggling.

I can't keep up with all the reading and writing. I slacked to the point of earning a C, and that wasn't normal for me. I put everything in me into my final paper, working countless hours to try to improve my grade. In the end, the professor congratulated me on my progress, and I was able to bump my grade to an A.

One of my final classes was Ethics, which was also hitting hard. I was put in a group for our final presentation about how sexuality and technology have changed what school is like for youths. I couldn't find much relevant content on the sexuality part, so instead, I discussed how technology has made information about sex more readily available to kids; how they could now find information about stuff they weren't necessarily talking about at home. But sex is a sensitive topic, especially with school-aged kids, so it's important to teach them how to find trustworthy sources to ensure they're getting safe, accurate information. The rest of the presentation, then, focused on the effective use of technology.

Every class seemed to focus heavily on research and writing, and it started to make my brain hurt. To me, college felt like jumping off a bridge, thinking the whole way that you aren't going to make it, but then you do. That was how I felt giving my final Ethics presentation. I was happy to find I was no longer scared or nervous. I felt prepared and accomplished, ready to take on whatever came at me next.

I was always grateful for my friendship with Star, even if we couldn't see each other as much as we both would have liked. But whenever we caught back up, it was like no time had passed at all. We made it a tradition to have lunch in the city whenever we saw each other. We both love a good brunch.

During one visit to NYC, our last before we'd graduate from college, she confessed that she'd gotten her first ever C in a class. I was shocked. I always had an image of her as an above average smart person, who never got anything other than A's. But college was brutal. We both knew that.

I figured it was my turn to confess. I told her I had

been seeing someone, someone I thought could be the one.

"Ela about your job, I know you want to work in the city, but I suggest you don't pass on any good opportunities," Star advised me, ignoring what I had just said. I nodded, knowing she was right. I'd made it so far with nothing but my own dreams and ambitions to consider. I needed to keep doing what was best for me. Somewhere along the way, Star had become my voice of reason. Once, on the train ride home from our brunch in New York City, we started arguing about me thinking that Alain was the one when I had just met him. We could never see eye to eye on the subject. Even still, we were always able to have the most open and genuine conversations in a healthy way. She was a safe space for me; I always felt heard.

Despite all the good books and shows she'd recommended, I'd never once been able to recommend something she loved. After reading The Giver and practically forcing her to read it, she said it could have been written better. In a lot of ways, I thought of Star as a sister. I knew she would always play a central role in my life, and

I knew I could depend on her no matter what.

HAVING HAD AN INTERNSHIP IN NEW YORK CITY WAS like a free pass on my resume. Even though I didn't gain much experience, I gained the privilege of having the big city name on my resume. I polished it off, and added it to the front of my portfolio before sending it to a job my friend Rene had rejected. I heard back almost immediately, which, to be fair, I should have taken that as a red flag.

Pau drove me to the interview, which was so hard to find I had to call the front desk twice and ask for directions. After driving in circles, we finally found the right place. I was greeted by Josh, the person I'd been in contact with about the job. He was an overly nice guy, wearing a flannel shirt tucked into his jeans. He directed me to a conference room located at the end of the open-floor office. The interview went well, and he offered me a job at $20 an hour. I told them I wasn't really willing to settle for anything less than $22 an hour, but thanked them anyway and said I'd be in touch with an answer.

On my way out, I couldn't help but notice all the tiny, messy cubicles. I should have taken it as another red flag, but I ignored it and left. The next day, Josh called and said that if I'd accept $20 an hour right now, I could be jumped up to $22 an hour after a three-month training period. Without knowing how bad of an idea that was, I accepted with no written agreement to rely on later. I knew it wasn't my dream job, but a full-time job in graphic design with a steady salary, benefits, and paid time off was too good to pass up.

With a stable job and income, I thought it was time to finally buy a car. I went to the dealership with my mother, though neither of us knew much about financing a car in the United States. I had to rely on the salesman to give me a good deal, though I didn't particularly care for him. He asked too many questions and was a little too comfortable with me for my liking.

I signed and signed and signed all the paperwork necessary. Finally, I was handed the key to my first car. Cherry, a little blue car that was truly a keeper. I felt like a woman, but more than that, I felt like I belonged. I felt like an immigrant success story, and I was proud of my heritage and how far I'd come. I knew I didn't have to be like anyone else to deserve to have basic needs met or a good life. I felt like I was home, even if to others, I was just an immigrant who deserves to just survive and not thrive.

Having a nine-to-five really made me feel like an adult. I changed the school schedule to night classes so I could finish my degree while working. The dress code was very laid back for a corporate space, but I was dressing for the job I wanted next, not the one I had. I've always been one of those people who wakes up really early when they're excited about something, so my first day I was up before 7:00am and had a lot of time to just chill out a bit. I arrived half an hour early. Nobody else was there yet, except for a quiet Chinese girl who directed me to my designated cubicle. I later learned that she was the snitch of the office, telling the boss everything she could think of as soon as she walked in the door.

My first day was strange. Mesmerized by the diversity that filled the room, I still couldn't identify with anybody. Josh introduced me to every staff member in the room, cubicle by cubicle. There was another woman starting that day in the finance department. The office restroom was all the way at the back of the warehouse, and you had to walk around towers of boxes just to access it. It seemed like the perfect place to be murdered quietly and without notice. The warehouse was ran by a Mexican man who always wore a hoodie. He was the only one I spoke to, mostly because everyone else seemed so unapproachable. However, that relationship quickly turned sour when he started messaging me repeatedly on Social Media, until I finally asked him to please stop.

Josh was the design director, and I had been hired on as his assistant designer. Josh spent the whole time complaining about everybody and gossiping about everyone there. It was irritating to know everyone's business so early in the onboarding process. But it was too late, no more time for red flags. I was in, and knew I would stay at least until I got my raise.

My second day was wild. One of the two people in HR was a new hire, and when I came in I heard the two screaming at each other until the new person stormed out. I never saw her again. I started to feel like I was going to be stuck in a job I hated.

The work I did there was fun, which balanced out the bad vibes. But Josh was a jerk. He micromanaged my every move, and it got to be rather exhausting. He constantly popped up behind me to look at my computer screen while I worked. Still, he had some tricks and skills I hadn't yet learned, so I was learning a lot. But he was stubborn, and I was constantly frustrated by how he so carelessly took credit for my work. I emailed Patrick hoping to commiserate, but he told me I should be flattered, that it was a good thing. Still, it didn't feel like a good thing. Josh was both hated and hateful, so he was constantly fighting with someone in the office. There was not a single day without an argument. My days were filled with doing work for which I would not be given credit. And, because of the close-knit leadership and borderline illegal family connections throughout the office, I couldn't even take my troubles to HR. I once had a school assignment out on my desk, and within minutes the HR lady was tapping me on the shoulder asking to speak to me in private. She said I shouldn't be doing school work here, and I apologized. But a few weeks later when I inquired about my raise, I was told I wouldn't be getting it because I wasn't as focused as I should be. They said I would get a raise upon graduating, but it felt like a major setback.

I figured I'd be fine. I knew that job was not my final destination anyway. The toxic environment was like a dark cloud hanging over my experience, reminding me why I shouldn't have been there to begin with. After five months, I noticed they were interviewing another designer. Josh had a habit of humiliating me in front of everyone, talking about how slow I was or how I could improve in certain areas. I would often run to the scary bathroom just for a moment of peace. Still, he told me not to worry about my job, that I was a good designer, and they were only hiring another person for extra help.

I was afraid to meet the new designer, Zak, but as soon as she walked through the door, we both knew we only had each other. I never told her about my experience so far, knowing she would eventually find things out on her own. After she joined the team, things became more bearable. We helped each other and were there for each other and, somehow, we both managed to survive.

I couldn't deny that I was becoming a more-well-rounded adult, and eventually, I was going to need to move out. With a new job and a new car, it was definitely the next logical step. I decided to move to a mid-sized house with four other people. When I broke the news to my mother, she was hesitant at first, but eventually, I received her blessing. I packed my life into plastic garbage bags and headed out on my own for the first time.

My first-time grocery shopping, I asked Alain to come along, but only as friends. He counted it as our second date. He was very complimentary, noting that he liked my street clothes, and I realized he had only ever seen me in work clothes. After we went shopping, I invited him to try my favorite Dominican foods, something I never get tired of. When I took him to see my favorite park, to hang out, he counted it as our third date. I found that I enjoyed his company, and enjoyed getting to know more about him. It felt like exchanging gifts every time we opened up another piece of our worlds to each other. I couldn't deny it. I was falling for him.

CHAPTER 12

PORTFOLIO PRESENTATION

I felt like I was finally living out my biggest dreams. Despite how much I doubted my ability to make it to this point, I finally felt like I was becoming who I was supposed to be. These thoughts invaded my head while I rested in the comfort of my bed. I've always been surrounded by hard-working people, so resting felt like a luxury. It all felt like it was moving so fast, and I was struggling to stay grounded. My body kept reminding me that I needed the rest, I didn't think I deserve. I tried focusing my eyes on my perfectly organized bookshelf, which stands firm to the left side of my bed, holding my most precious possessions. My books. I concentrated on each one, trying to bring myself back to the time I read each one, trying to feel the emotions they evoked in me. It calmed me down but also made me think of the books waiting and wondering if I'd ever pick them up.

I took a deep breath, breathing in all the oxygen in the room, letting the good memories wash over me. I focused on how much I'd accomplished, the good memories, and how much they meant to me. With each exhale, I released the self-doubt and worry that had plagued me for so long. I laid there for a while, wondering if this is what freedom felt like.

It was my last semester, and just three classes stood between me and my degree. Handling this new life I tried to play it off by not eating at my mom's house. I cooked for a month before I was back, carrying out mom's menu in Tupperware containers. But I still couldn't escape the financial burden. It seemed like every semester I was battling the financial aid office trying to get things resolved. And this semester was no different.

The new director of the graphic design department, Mr. Smith, prepared a real-world assignment for us. He set up mock interviews, and we'd all take turns sitting with each other and honing our interview skills. He pre-pared a list of questions for us each to ask, but the spon-taneity of the situation made my anxiety go through the roof.

I was paired with another student, and I worried that he wouldn't be able to understand me. My accent aside, the nerves I was feeling made my voice sound weak and shakey. I was happy to have the practice. The whole exercise made me realize that I needed it.

We also worked on preparing our portfolios to present to the rest of the professors in the department. I searched back through all my past projects, and it was like taking a look back in time. I couldn't help but remember the feeling that I didn't belong, and some of that was even reflected in my early work. But as time went on, I got better, and so did my work. I no longer felt the need to hide. Not myself, and certainly not my work.

I printed out a few of my best pieces to include in the portfolio. I was both nervous and excited to present. It was thrilling to have finally made it to the end.

After school, I had planned to hang out with Alain. At first, our dates seemed like one more item on my to-do list, but I found myself really enjoying his company. He was always surprising me with romantic gestures. For our last date, he showed up with sunflowers, my favorite. I practically melted. Though I didn't see it coming, I realized I was ready to introduce him to my friends and family. I guess I was starting to feel serious about him,

after all, he's been there even before we had our first official first date.

CHAPTER 13

ADULTING-ISH

Because I didn't know how whether or not my move was permanent, I never changed my address and still got mail delivered to my mom's house. Though I didn't want to admit it, it was mostly just an excuse for me to have to go there regularly. I went most days after school, letting myself in with the keys I practically refused to give up. Once, while in the elevator, I ran into my old neighbor. He was an older man, and the crow's feet around his eyes were proof that he'd lived a happy life. I missed running into him and was happy to hear that he had missed me, too.

"I have to feel like an adult," I told him. He smirked and told me that he knew my sisters and I were made for great things. I got off the elevator and walked to my family's apartment. Everyone was home, which I knew they would be. Every time I come in my mom and sisters and I regroup and catch each other up on what we've been doing. Whenever they heard my voice, they'd start to gather in whichever room I chose. It seemed all we talked about anymore was Alain, even though I didn't have much to update them on because we were still just "friends".

"You've got mail," my mom said, handing me an already opened letter. I was thinking about scolding her for the illegality of opening someone else's mail when I realized it was a letter from school. The envelope said it was from the financial aid office, but I thought it was insignificant. I had already dealt with that office so many times, I thought it couldn't be anything new. I unfolded the letter and read:

Dear Rafaela,

We regret to inform you that your loans were not successfully processed due to insufficient paperwork. Because the deadline has passed, we will be unable to provide funding for the current semester. Please visit the student accounts office immediately…

It seemed like I couldn't make it through a single semester without an issue with my financial aid, but this time was different. I was worried. I rescheduled my date with Alain so I could take time to process, and made a plan to go to the financial aid office first thing the next day.

When I got to the accounts office the next day, I was vainly hoping that my account would be clear and the absurd letter was just a mistake. I had been to the office so many times before that I started to think of the middle-aged woman who handled my account as a personal friend. She approached me, using the same welcoming tone I had gotten used to. She asked for my ID and I handed it to her, determined on getting the matter resolved.

She sat down in front of the computer, and I felt like my heart was racing in tandem with her fingers on the keyboard. "Miss, you have an outstanding balance of $11,000 dollar. How would you like to pay?" She asked cynically.

I was frustrated, both by her words and by the situation. I had been there so many times before, I couldn't believe no one had thought to bring this up sooner.

Suddenly, it hit me. The weight of that letter finally

sunk in, and I knew I needed to get myself out of the debt owed. I needed to pay it in full in order to graduate and receive my diploma. I composed myself and told her I didn't have the money to pay right away. I went into problem-solving mode and asked her for alternatives. I asked about installments, but she said that even if I planned to pay off the debt long-term I still wouldn't be able to walk with my classmates or receive my diploma. I was even more frustrated than I was before, and I could feel the tears falling from my eyes. Still, I mumbled a thank you and left the office crying. "I'm so–" I turned away before she could finish her sentence. Walking out of the office I ran into Rene, who asked me what was wrong. I told her not to worry and kept walking.

I drove to my family's house to break the news to them. They were as sad and confused as I was, but they immediately started to plan it all out, trying to come up with a way we could get the money together. But gradu-ation was just a month away, and that kind of money felt entirely impossible. Despite the "adulthood" lifestyle I was adopting, I was still just a 21-year-old trying to make ends meet. The world of credit and lending was sadly very foreign to me, so the idea of opening a credit card to pay tuition was just as scary as anything else. I let my fear and anxiety take over, and I just gave up.

I was in disbelief that I had given so much of myself to the school—my time, my mental health, course work and everything else—and they still had the power to deny me of the finality of it all, just like that. I saw the other face of the American school system. I felt betrayed like I was nothing but a paycheck to them, and they didn't actually care about whether or not I received a quality education. I decided to go home and just not think about anything for a while I knew there had to be a solution, but it was hard to get past the sadness of knowing I wouldn't be walking at graduation with my classmates. When I got home, I went straight to my room, thankful that none of my roommates were home. I couldn't socialize with them or anyone else. I closed my door and laid down on my bed, letting the tears flow as long and hard as they needed. I was tired, and though I knew I wasn't ready to give up, I was aware that I was up against something much more powerful than myself.

After a while, I picked up my phone to scroll through

the recent notifications. A few junk emails, a message from my sisters and one from Alain. I noticed a message from the Dean of the Graphic Design department telling me he might have a solution to my problem and to hang in there. Another from Rene telling me that she had heard what happened and went to the Dean to try to work out a deal. I started to feel hopeful, and thankful to have the support of so many. All I could do was wait and see.

The next morning, I tried to move past it all. When my alarm went off, I hit the snooze button a few times before finally getting up to get ready for work. I put on my favorite playlist and let my favorite tracks fill the space around me. I was definitely feeling better, hopeful that the Dean, at least, would be able to help me. I dressed for work and had breakfast, then headed out into a brilliantly sunny morning. I thought the day might turn out all right after all. When I got outside, I noticed one of my pay stubs on the ground. I bent to pick it up, thinking I must have dropped it the night before. But then I noticed the broken glass on the ground, and when I got to my car I could see it was from my drivers-side window.

I was furious. I felt helpless and small in a world that seemed determined to swallow me whole. In truth, I wasn't mad about the vandalism, I was mad about the timing of it. I felt like I couldn't take one more thing.

I didn't think I had anything of value in the car, so I didn't bother with a police report. I called the insurance company so they'd pay for the repair, and I called the office to let them know I'd be coming in late. Thankfully, I was able to drive to a repair shop and have the window repaired while I waited.

The auto shop was in a beautiful, rural setting, surrounded by green fields and clean air. Despite it all, it was a beautiful day, so I decided to take a walk while I waited. I couldn't help but wonder if all the struggle I was facing would really be worth the reward. But, I moved forward with the faith that if there was a problem, there also had to be a solution.

I received a call that my car was ready. I walked to the front desk, and when the lady asked for payment, I couldn't help but laugh internally. Another woman at a desk, asking for money I didn't have. Thankfully, I had been saving up for next month's rent, so I had what I needed in my account. I just hoped the insurance compa-

ny would reimburse me in time to make rent. A mechan-

ic came out to hand me my keys. He wished me a good

day, and I took off to head to work. On the way there, I

played some music, trying to picture a near future where

all of this would be okay.

CHAPTER 14

A CONFETTI-FILLED DAY

Everyday after work, it had become a habit to call my mother. We always had something to talk about, to the extent that we were rarely able to finish a conversation. It was often very casual, but also sometimes meant walking her through the strange series of events happening to me. But one day, instead of calling her, I called Alain. It had been a few days since we'd seen each other, and I was really starting to miss him.

When we spoke, I told him everything that was going on, and his initial reaction was to help in any way he could. He said we could work together to come up with a plan for the money, but I told him I needed to figure it out on my own. "I understand," he said. "Would you like to meet and talk about this?" I could hear the hesitation in his voice, but I knew I needed to do this for myself.

"Sorry, it's just not a good time. But I will reach out soon." I said.

We hung up, and, though I was sad, it felt good knowing I had his support.

The drive back home from work was depressing. I felt so helpless and powerless. I was telling myself everything was going to work out, but it was hard to believe my own words. I was lost in my own thoughts, when suddenly the music stopped and my phone started ringing. It was the Dean of the Graphic Design program. I took a deep breath and answered.

"Hello?" I said, my voice quiet and shaky.

"Rafaela, I'm so sorry, but there's nothing we can do so that you can still walk on graduation day. I spoke with the school President, and unfortunately, there are some rules we just can't change." I could tell by his tone that he was being genuine and honest, and I was appreciative of him for trying.

"Thank you for trying," I said. I had no other words.

"I sent you a list of private loans that you can apply for. Good luck."

I was touched that he had taken so much time to help solve my problems, but the chances of me getting approved for a private loan felt slim. But it was my only option, and I realized I'd have to set my fears aside if I wanted to walk at graduation so I considered applying for a loan.

When I arrived home, I was disappointed. I was angry. But more than anything else, I was exhausted. I carried my tired body up to my bedroom and laid down, shutting my eyes for a while and trying to relax.

After a while, I unlocked my phone to check my notifications. There was an email from my school's president, a farewell message to graduates. I couldn't help but see it as a slap in the face. He was pretending to care, but I knew what we all were to him; paychecks. One section, in particular, caught my eye. He asked us to reach out to him to let him know of our experience. Without thinking, I poured my days of frustration and hurt into an email to him and sent it off. I thought that, at least if he couldn't let me walk, he should know how much it hurt me. It wasn't what I wanted, but it felt good to let my anger run free.

I was surprised when he responded so quickly, apologizing for the confusion and encouraging me to apply for a private loan. I felt even angrier like he'd missed my point entirely. He was the one person with the power to help, and he didn't. I never replied.

I had dealt with so much that day, so I put on my comfiest pajamas and went downstairs to make myself a cup of tea. While I waited for it to cool, I opened my laptop and browsed through the private loan options everyone had been sending me. A few actually look promising, and I started to think that maybe borrowing money wouldn't be so bad if it meant I'd get to experience graduation in the way I wanted to. Eventually, I selected a loan and applied. Then all I could do was wait.

The next day, I woke up to my alarm and immediately grabbed my phone to check my email, hoping for an approval notice from the lending company, but there was no word. That day was graduation picture day, so I packed my cap and gown in my bag, thinking I would just move through everything as planned. I felt optimistic, which made me feel oddly pathetic. Still, I had worked hard to be where I was, and I wasn't going to let anything ruin the pride I was feeling in myself.

I had a few texts asking for updates on the situation—from Star, Alain, and my sisters. But I had nothing new to report, so I didn't answer them right away. I met up with my classmates, all of whom seemed to know what was happening with my loan eligibility. I explained the situation while we waited to have our photos taken, thankful for the sympathy that I knew they truly felt. When my turn came for a photo, I was elated. Standing there, wearing my cap and gown, it all felt right. I was unbothered by my situation, just thankful to have made it as far as I did. When the flash went off, I imagined the photo would be in all my relative's homes in the Dominican Republic, how they'd point to it when their friends were over and tell them how proud they were of me. My whole life up to that point, visible in a 5"x7" frame on the mantle.

Afterward, I decided to stop by Dunkin' Donuts for some rum raisin ice cream. But really, I was wishing to see Alain. It wasn't his local Dunkin', but it kind of became our place. He had been back a few times since, so I thought there was a chance he'd be there.

I checked my phone every minute, hoping to see an email about my loan application. Each time I can't help but see the graduation invitations on my purse and it's terrifying to think I'd never even use them.

Finally, an email came through. I could only imagine that it could be good news. It had to be good news, because I couldn't bear any more disappointment, and it was my last chance to receive my diploma. I opened the email with shaking hands, momentarily losing focus because of the fear and excitement that was hitting me all at once.

I was approved. I laid my head on the table, not able to remain upright as the relief washed over me. After the last few weeks, I needed this news. It was finally over. I was doing it. I was excited to break the news to my family, but I stayed at Dunkin' for a while, still hoping Alain would show up. My schedule had become predictable, and I thought he must know I was there.

I was just sitting there, basking in my good news when I suddenly felt a tap on my shoulder and jumped. There he was; Alain. He was smiling sweetly at me, and I returned the smile and told him how happy I was to see him. We sat in silence for a while, just staring at each other, having a silent conversation that communicated so much. I knew just looking at him how glad he was to see me, and I hoped he understood how sorry I was for leaving him hanging for so long.

I reached into my purse and pulled out a graduation

invitation and handed it to him. He laughed, tilting his head back and looking at the ceiling. "I knew you could do it," he said. He looked at the invitation, read through all the information about graduation. We sat in silence for a while longer, just staring at each other, letting our months of togetherness catch up to us all at once.

Suddenly, he stood and came around to my side of the table. I stood to meet him and his hand found my chin, tilting my face up toward his so our eyes met. Slowly, he brought his mouth down to mine and kissed me. Hard. I knew everything I needed to know about us. I knew we were an us.

A FEW DAYS LATER, ALAIN AND I WENT TO THE MALL to pick out a dress for graduation. I had so much fun trying on dresses with him, feeling beautiful every time I opened a dressing room door and showed him the next option. Somewhere in the midst of our little fashion show, I got a text from my sister Pam.

Pam twin: I'm proud of you!

A simple text, but it still made me incredibly emotional. It felt great knowing that someone so close to me, who knew me and saw me through these major life transitions, was proud of me. I had been so focused on what was next, graduate school or a promotion or a new job, that I hadn't really stopped to celebrate my current achievements. Her message was a reminder to slow down and enjoy the moment.

"Hey, I have to do something real quick, stay here," Alain said. I smiled internally, realizing for the first time how bad he is at surprises.

GRADUATION DAY WAS EVERYTHING I IMAGINED IT WOULD BE. Despite the heavy rain that ruined my hair and the impassable traffic we were stuck in just trying to get to the school, I was overjoyed. All I could think about was my friends and family, how they'd get to watch me achieve this huge milestone. I thought of Alain, potentially the greatest love of my life, and how much he cared for me. It was everything I'd hoped for and more.

The line of students waiting to file into their seats was long, but it gave me the chance to hug all my friends one last time and wish them well before their own new adventures would begin. They all looked so radiant and successful.

The graduation song finally sounded, and we all made our way to our seats. My eyes went right to my loved ones. I couldn't believe how amazing it felt having them all there to see my biggest accomplishment yet. It wasn't just about me. It was about them, too. We did this together.

I thought about aunt Celania, the first of our family to make it to the states. She often had to sleep in apartment lobbies, clutching her luggage and hoping no one would mess with her in the night. I thought of my grandparents and the hours and hours of hard work they endured trying to save enough money to bring my mother here. I thought of my sisters and the opportunities they had, the opportunities I had. I thought of our family's future and the generations that would come next. We had made it so far, and I was so proud and joyful.

The ceremony ended, and confetti rained down on us from the ceilings. It was done. I did it.

At that moment, Alain appeared by my side. "I couldn't wait to congratulate you and give you your gift," he said, pulling a little black box from his pocket.

I immediately started to freak out. "No," I said. "No no no no no." I was shaking my head in disbelief. Though I knew I was capable of loving Alain, I wasn't ready for this.

"WAIT," he shouted. "It's not *that*. Just open it!"

I took the box from him and opened it. I couldn't believe my eyes. Inside was a silver Mickey Mouse ring. I looked at it with watery eyes. I couldn't believe that from all our conversations he remembered the friendship ring I had to give up in school because I didn't have the money to buy my high school graduation dress. I completely forgot I'd shared this with him.

CHAPTER 15

GIRL BRUNCH THINGS

Pam and Pau asked me to meet them for lunch the day after graduation. We were on very different paths with entirely different personalities, but nothing in the world was better than the relationship the three of us had. We feed off each other, always able to offer comfort or a joke or just the quiet kindness of good company. No one in the world knows me as my sisters do, and I've always been thankful for that.

When I pulled up to the restaurant, they were already there waiting for me. I found it unusual. But what was even more unusual was a suitcase with a bow occupying one of the seats at the table. Many exciting questions popped up in my head, but I just wanted to know: Where? Where? Where might we be going? They wouldn't tell me anything and it was making me anxious, but the good kind of anxious.

We ordered our meals and ate our food. I ordered dessert because, well, they had already said they were paying.

Rushing through the last bite of my strawberry-topped flan, I demanded they finally tell me what they were up to. They loved keeping this secret from me, sitting back with their cool composure while I fell to pieces with excitement. I was ready to grab my suitcase and go wherever they wanted me to. I could see them trying to keep me in suspense a few moments longer, but finally, they had to let it out.

"We're taking you to the D.R. and we leave in a week!" They said it at the same time, their excitement barely contained.

"Oh…" I said quietly. "That's great. Thank you." I tried to sound excited but I couldn't. Their eyes met, and I could tell they were both put off by my reaction. They wanted me to be more excited but I wasn't, and they wanted to know why.

Why wasn't I more excited? I also wanted to know. The thought of traveling back home came with a mix of confusing feelings. The thought of traveling back home takes my body back to a place where it doesn't feel safe, protected, or cared for, it's like going to a war field, and it just doesn't feel appropriately equipped to defend itself.

"Here is the thing," I managed to say. I don't know why here, at a Colombian restaurant full of people, right now is where I feel strong enough. Or, in reality, I feel weak enough, vulnerable enough, tired of carrying around the weight of my history of sexual abuse. Right now, I hear my body speak; I hear it, I don't shut down the distress it's been carrying. I let it grieve. I let it grieve what it's lost. I validated its pain. This has gotten too heavy, and I don't want to carry it out alone. If I decided to go, we would need a bigger suitcase because this one isn't big enough to hold the things I'd have to bring with me. Being able to share that I was the victim of child sexual abuse filled me with relief. Sharing my story was like validating its existence, validating the existence of that six-year-old girl who had made it through so much. I needed an outlet, and they were giving it to me

Suddenly, I didn't feel as though I was there with my sisters. I was back in the D.R., heading towards that old outdoor bathroom. I open the door and she's there, a little girl that was abandoned, betrayed, and left with nothing but her own darkness. I bring with me what I think she needs the most. A pink dress that she loved. A soft white towel. Shea butter that will be gentle against her bruised skin. I bring gentleness itself. I embrace her, wishing the pain was transferable, wishing I could rid us both of it. I make sure she knows that even though someone picked her up and threw her in the fire, she's now being held by people that would walk into burning flames for her. I hold her in my arms a little longer, until I restore in her a life she wants to live. I hit all the light switches in her. I bring her back to life and plan to lay with her for as long as she needs me to. I went to grab her favorite ice cream, *Helados Bon*, which she still loves so much, it's not her birthday, but the culture would allow it for her. Just for her.

I fear for her companionship because not even for a second do I want her to feel alone. I don't know how to help her, not when she's so fragile, but I know that some-day she can feel whole again. I'll move mountains if I have to. I'll break stigmas; I'll break the culture for her.

My entire life has been pain, revolving around the de-cisions other people made for me. But not anymore. Now I know that I am strong, and I can bring my own joy and happiness into my life.

ACKNOWLEDGEMENTS

I'm grateful to God for allowing me to walk on earth with a purpose that keeps my soul alive.

ABOUT THE AUTHOR

Sindy Feliz was born in the Dominican Republic in 1994. She holds a Bachelor's degree in Fine Arts and is the author of the anthology *Go Inspire*. She's the creator of the *Return the Love* box, created to help improve the quality of education and provide resources for Clara Rosa Perez primary school, Los Patos.

🌐 sindyf.com

✉ contact@sindyf.com

📷 sindyfe_